Children of the Mist

Also by Bill Knox

The Thane and Moss police series:
Deadline for a Dream (1957)
Death Department (1959)
Leave it to the Hangman (1960)
Little Drops of Blood (1962)
Sanctuary Isle (1962)
The Man in the Bottle (1963)
The Taste of Proof (1965)
The Deep Fall (1966)
Justice on the Rocks (1967)
The Tallyman (1968)
To Kill a Witch (1971)
Draw Batons (1973)
Rally to Kill (1975)
Pilot Error (1977)
Live Bait (1978)
A Killing in Antiques (1981)
The Hanging Tree (1983)
The Crossfire Killings (1986)
The Interface Man (1989)
The Counterfeit Killers (1996)
Blood Proof (1997)
Death Bytes (1998)
The Lazarus Widow (1999)

The Webb Carrick fishery
protection series:
The Scavengers (1964)
Devilweed (1966)
Blacklight (1967)
The Klondyker (1968)
Blueback (1969)
Seafire (1970)
Stormtide (1972)
Whitewater (1974)
Hellspout (1976)
Witchrock (1977)
Bombship (1980)
Bloodtide (1982)
Wavecrest (1985)
Dead Man's Mooring (1987)
The Drowning Nets (1991)

Other crime fiction as Bill Knox:
The Cockatoo Crime (1958)
Death Calls the Shots (1961)
Die for Big Betsy (1961)

With Edward Boyd:
The View from Daniel Pike (1974)

Non-fiction:
*Court of Murder: Famous trials at
Glasgow High Court (1968)*
Tales of Crime (1982)

Written as Robert Macleod
Talos Cord investigator series:
The Drum of Power (1964)
Cave of Bats (1964)
Lake of Fury (1966)
Isle of Dragons (1967)
Place of Mists (1969)
Path of Ghosts (1971)
Nest of Vultures (1973)

Jonathan Gaunt 'Remembrancer'
series:
A Property in Cyprus (1970)
A Killing in Malta (1972)
A Burial in Portugal (1973)
A Witchdance in Bavaria (1975)
A Pay-off in Switzerland (1977)
An Incident in Iceland (1979)
A Problem in Prague (1981)
A Legacy from Tenerife (1984)
A Cut in Diamonds (1985)
The Money Mountain (1987)
The Spanish Maze Game (1990)

Andrew Laird marine insurance
series:
All Other Perils (1974)
Dragonship (1976)
Salvage Job (1978)
Cargo Risk (1980)
Mayday From Malaga (1983)
Witchline (1988)

CHILDREN
OF THE MIST

Bill Knox

Constable • London

Constable & Robinson Ltd
3 The Lanchesters
162 Fulham Palace Road
London W6 9ER
www.constablerobinson.com

First published in Great Britain 1970
This edition published in Great Britain by Constable,
an imprint of Constable & Robinson Ltd 2005

A copy of the British Library Cataloguing in Publication
Data is available from the British Library.

ISBN 1-84529-127-1

Printed and bound in the EU

Chapter One

They call Clover Glen's 130-yard thirteenth hole 'Coronary Hill'. A low tee, usually waterlogged, stares up at a high plateau which is guarded by deep sandtrap bunkers and crowned by a handkerchief-sized green. Depending on wind and weather the approach needs anything between a seven iron and a full drive. Then comes the climb up that grassy Eiger . . . impatient candidates on the club waiting list bless the hill each winter, apprehensive older members campaign for a stretcher to be placed somewhere near.

The wind was moderate and from the west in the early grey world of that damp Wednesday morning in January. In off-duty tartan wool shirt, canary yellow sweater and grubby whipcord slacks, Detective Chief Inspector Colin Thane muttered to himself and scowled up towards the green.

He guessed a five iron should be enough. Not that it probably mattered much which club he chose. The kind of golf he'd been producing made him glad there were no witnesses around.

In fact, as far as he knew he was the only golfer out so early. Which in turn was mainly due to the incompetent idiocy of a safe-blowing ned named Harry-Boy Tait. This time the fatally incompetent idiocy – when Tait had chosen the ungodly hour of 3 a.m. that morning to blast open a jeweller's strongroom in King Street he'd been careless, downright reckless about the size of charge for the lob.

The bang had shattered every window within a hundred

5

yards. The crew of a patrol car answered the emergency call, found what remained of Harry-Boy – and within fifteen minutes Thane's bedside telephone was ringing.

Identifying the body hadn't been easy. And the City Mortuary before dawn rated low in terms of comfort even without such incidentals as Doc Williams, the police surgeon, being in a state of sleepy-eyed ill temper.

One way and another it had been a miserable start to what, in theory, was a rest-day for the head of Millside Division C.I.D. When Colin Thane finally arrived home again it was after eight and Mary was getting the kids ready for school. Any thought of going back to bed was extinguished within moments. It was already occupied by the family hound who growled indignantly at the mere suggestion of being moved.

He'd cursed the animal for a four-legged layabout then settled for breakfast and early golf.

Which, inevitably, included the short thirteenth. Thane took the five iron, teed the ball high, and prepared to swing. A flicker of movement off to the right caught the corner of his eye and the swing became a slice. He swore as the ball performed a near vertical take-off then plummeted into the rough.

'Hard luck.' The loud, cheerful comment came from an all too familiar figure now loping towards the tee. Oblivious of his offence, the lanky young man arrived and greeted him with a grin. 'I'd say you raised your head, sir. It's easily done.'

'Maybe.' Not for the first time Colin Thane decided that life would be a lot easier if he could have Detective Constable Beech transferred out of Millside Division. Into the Mounted Branch, for instance. As a horse, for preference. He sighed and leaned on the club. 'Well, what's wrong now?'

'Nothing desperate, sir. At least I don't think so. Chief Superintendent Ilford wants you at Headquarters for a meeting. The message came into Division about half an

6

hour ago.' Beech glanced around with interest. 'Enjoying your game?'

'I was.' Thane regarded him stonily. 'What kind of meeting?'

'He didn't say.' Beech gave the kind of shrug which meant junior detective constables didn't quiz chief super-intendents. 'I phoned your home and your wife said you were playing so – well, here I am.'

'Thanks.' Grimly, Thane shoved the club back into his dilapidated golf bag, found his cigarettes and lit one. 'When's the meeting?'

'Just as soon as you can get there, sir.' Beech gestured in the direction of the clubhouse. 'I brought the duty car.'

Thane nodded reluctantly, considering. First he'd need a shave and a change of clothes. Second, playing in from the thirteenth towards the clubhouse wasn't too much of a variation from a straight line back. Not if you hit the ball properly. And third, the average Headquarters conference was seldom really urgent.

Mind made up, he dragged out the five iron again and shoved the golf bag into Beech's hands.

'Sir?' Beech blinked uncertainly.

'Promotion,' said Thane bleakly. 'Caddy for me.'

His second ball off the tee rose high and straight – before it tailed and vanished into the depths of the main sandtrap.

For once, Detective Constable Beech had sense enough to keep his mouth shut.

Glasgow police headquarters is a big, grey and old-fashioned building in St Andrews Street. That's near enough to the city centre for most purposes yet sufficiently far from the business and shopping mainstreams to avoid too frequent a reminder of its existence – the overcrowded, overworked heart of a network of police divisions, a net-work handling over 45,000 crime incidents a year plus another 60,000 items vaguely labelled 'miscellaneous offences'.

7

Colin Thane arrived shortly before 11 a.m. The Millside Division duty car double-parked briefly outside the main entrance to let him out then nosed off in search of a permanent stopping place.

Once inside the building Thane stopped in the lobby to check with the inquiry desk orderly. He was directed up to the second floor conference room, usually Administration territory. Raising a surprised eyebrow he ignored the elevator and headed up the stairway.

He always did, preferring the exercise, conscious that he'd put on a few pounds since the time when he'd been a beat cop and an amateur heavyweight boxer – the kind of amateur who'd finally become tired of being regularly knocked out in semi-finals.

But he still moved with the smooth, muscular ease of an athlete. And pretty well looked the part. Nudging forty, topping the six foot mark, Colin Thane had close-clipped dark hair and a tanned face which could be politely classed as pleasantly rugged. When it came to police work the best label to describe his methods was that they constituted a mixture of impetuous hope and consciously applied effort.

Somehow it usually worked, which was why he rated as youngest of the city's chief inspectors – with C.I.D. command of one of the toughest, most awkward divisions.

Thane reached the conference room with a gathering wisp of concern about whether he'd under-rated this particular summons. But the door was ajar, he could hear voices coming from behind its frosted glass, and there was only one way to find out. He smoothed the pocket flaps of his grey Donegal tweed suit, took a deep breath, knocked briefly, and entered.

The room was smoke-filled. Several coffee cups lay around the long table. But only two of the chairs were still occupied.

'Better late than never. Come on in, Thane.' Rising bulkily to his feet and in reasonably good humour, Chief Super-

8

intendent William 'Buddha' Ilford, head of the city's C.I.D. force, beckoned with a large hand. The second man was tall and rake-thin with a small dark moustache. He wore police uniform, the custom-tailored variety with Assistant Chief Constable's epaulettes. But he was a stranger.

'Formalities first,' declared Ilford, turning towards the stranger. 'Archie, this is your man. Thane, this is Mr Meikle – he's an Assistant Chief with the Perth County force. He's been talking with a few of us.'

Meikle smiled, but only with his lips. His handshake was light and formal.

'Sit down,' instructed Ilford. He flopped back into his chair, waited till the others had followed his example, and said suddenly, 'Any problems about that idiot who blew himself up last night?'

'No, sir.' Thane sensed their visitor was inspecting him with a particular care and began to wonder what was shaping.

'Good. And the rest of Millside Division seems fairly quiet right now, judging by your crime returns.' Ilford gave a brief, significant glance towards the other man. 'Archie?'

Meikle built a slow church steeple with his long, thin fingers then cleared his throat delicately.

'Ever been up around the Braedale area, Chief Inspector?'

Thane nodded. 'A few times, sir. Mostly passing through, going north with the family on holiday.'

Probably most people tagged Braedale as a place they'd passed through. Colin Thane had a vague memory of rich green fields and one hot summer day when he'd stopped at a village pub for a long glass of ice-cold lager. Situated in the north of Perth county, it was farming territory, mostly cattle rearing. Just beyond began the blue-grey bulk of the Grampian Mountains.

Meikle relaxed a little. 'Any friends or relatives up there, Thane?'

9

'None, sir.'

Apparently satisfied, the man nodded and sank back.

There was another long silence. Buddha Ilford stuffed tobacco into the bowl of his aluminium-stemmed pipe but laid it aside unlit. Sitting deep in his chair, the C.I.D. chief's eyes strayed down to contemplate the area around his navel – the attitude of sleepy thought which had earned him his nickname.

'The Perthshire force has a problem at Braedale,' said Ilford at last. 'It's the kind the book says needs an independent investigating officer. That's going to be you, Colin. It'll mean going up for a few days.' He caught the protest shaping on Thane's lips and beat him to it with a rumbling authority. 'No arguments. As far as Millside's concerned I'll draft in Hertson to keep your chair warm. He's doing nothing.'

Thane fought down a wince. Chief Inspector Hertson was spare to Central Division, an acid-tongued veteran close to retiral age. The last time he'd deputized at Millside the result had been a near mutiny.

'Couldn't Hertson . . .'

'No.' Ilford shook his head. 'Hertson's low on tact. You're not much better, I'll agree. But you've a politer brand of insolence – and there's another reason. You're on the National Crime Squad reserve list and it's that kind of job.'

Resignedly, Thane watched while Ilford struck a match and got the pipe's tobacco going.

'There's been a killing, a fairly unusual one.' Ilford said it between puffs, his voice matter-of-fact but an odd glint in his eyes. 'The Perthshire force need help from outside for one very simple reason. The main suspect happens to be the local police inspector.'

That altered things, altered them a lot. Thane gave a soft, appreciative whistle and rubbed a thumb along his chin.

'Who's been killed?'

'Not who. The word is "what",' corrected Ilford. 'The

answer is a bull by the name of Marquis of Braedale, aged sixteen months, weight approximately half a ton. It was found shot dead yesterday morning. The local vet held a p.m. and dug a .38 bullet out of the brute's brain.'

Thane stared at him.

'A bull,' emphasized Ilford with what came close to sympathy. 'But get rid of any idea that the world has gone crazy. This bull happened to be pretty special.'

'The Marquis was one of the best young Black Angus breeding bulls ever reared,' said Meikle wearily. 'He belonged to a pedigree breeder named Adam Jennings. Two months ago Jennings sold the Marquis to a Texas cattle syndicate. The price was 120,000 dollars to be paid on delivery.'

'Live delivery,' emphasized Ilford. He waved an expressive hand. 'So the deal died with the Marquis. Jennings is fairly lucky – he had the animal insured under one of those standard bull-breeder policies, so he doesn't lose everything. But the result is still one hell of an expensive chunk of prime beefsteak.'

Somehow, Thane managed a nod and tried to get the thing into perspective. Suppose there had been – well, near enough a £50,000 arson job in his division and one of the Millside team had been implicated. Yes, Assistant Chief Constable Meikle had plenty of reason to be unhappy.

He glanced at the County man. 'The local man, sir?'

'Inspector Fenn,' replied Meikle gloomily. 'Charles Rennie Fenn, fifteen years' service, good record but hotheaded. He and Jennings have been feuding for months, enough for Jennings to have complained to Headquarters he was being victimized.'

'And was he?'

'The evidence didn't add up to anything. But after that plenty of people heard Fenn swear he'd hit Jennings where it would hurt.' Meikle reached under the table and brought out a briefcase. 'The time of death for the bull is reckoned as about 1 a.m. – that's the post mortem calculation. The body wasn't found till morning, and we've three basic facts. Jennings had some sort of committee meeting going on at his home that night and it didn't break up till around 1.30 a.m. But at a little after 1 a.m. a farmhand claims he saw someone who he says looked like Fenn walking away from the farmyard area. And at one-twenty Fenn was positively identified as being the driver of a car heading away from the farm.'

'This "positive" identification, sir – a reliable witness?'

'Witnesses – and you couldn't ask for better. His own sergeant and a constable. They were in a patrol car, on their way to a road accident.' Opening the briefcase, Meikle drew out a thin manilla folder. It slid across the table towards Thane. 'That's the file to date, which isn't much. I got to Braedale about noon yesterday. As soon as I saw how things were shaping I ordered a complete halt to local investigation – particularly after I'd seen Fenn at his home. I wanted to give him a chance to talk. Instead, he practically threw me out on my ear.'

'How to win friends,' murmured Thane. 'And your own view, sir?'

'My view doesn't matter a damn. What happens next depends on your official report.'

'Which we'll want quickly,' grunted Ilford. He sucked his pipe again then used the stem as a warning pointer. 'Fenn's popular with his men. Don't expect particularly willing help. And forget he's a cop, Colin. That's where the real trouble can lie.'

'True.' Closing the briefcase, Meikle got to his feet with unconcealed relief. 'That's it, then – time I was leaving.'

'Now?' Ilford glanced at his watch. 'I'd planned on our Chief buying us lunch, Archie.'

'Sorry – I've got to get back.' Meikle began moving towards the door then stopped. 'Thane, I'll give you another item of advice. Adam Jennings is a Nationalist – Home Rule for Scotland, English Go Home, all the rest of it. He's so much of a fanatic the National Party chucked him out. That part is in the file. What isn't is this. Jennings runs a Home Rule splinter party with a lot of youngsters clinging to the edges. One of them is Charlie Fenn's daughter. If there's any real reason for the feud between Jennings and Fenn that's it – whatever else you hear.'

He frowned as if he'd said more than he meant, nodded, and the door closed with a slam as he left.

'Well?' queried Ilford from behind a cloud of pipe smoke. 'What do you think of it?'

'He's worried,' mused Thane. 'And taking it pretty personally.'

'Uh-huh.' Ilford scratched behind one ear. 'Maybe because he personally recommended Fenn for promotion to inspector – and got him shipped out to Braedale when the same Fenn was in a rumpus about a year back. Even an Assistant Chief can find his head on the chopping block.' He chuckled a little. 'Anyway, I told him you'd need this afternoon to sort things out. But get to Braedale tonight. I want you working there by first thing tomorrow. Any notion where you'll start?'

'By reading this, I suppose.' Thane tapped the file wryly. 'What about transport, sir?'

'We'll lay on a car to take you up. Then the County will provide all facilities.' Ilford ruminated for a moment. 'If this idiot Fenn really did shoot the Marquis there's going to be trouble spreading in several directions. You'd better have some decent support from here, just in case. I can't spare anyone from Headquarters' – he pipe-sucked again then decided – 'better take Phil Moss with you. If he moans, tell him there's nothing like a few farmyard smells to tune up a man.'

Thane grinned. Detective Inspector Moss, his second-in-command at Millside, would have his own comment on that one.

'Right.' Ilford glanced at his watch again and grimaced. 'Well, no free lunch now. But I've a better idea. Phone Moss and tell him to pack a bag. Then we can go and have

13

a sandwich and a beer somewhere. We'll make it a beef sandwich and call it basic research.'

Thane had another name for it. If the day ever dawned when Buddha Ilford bought his own lunch a shock wave would ripple through the Headquarters building.

It took a minute or so to locate Phil Moss when he telephoned Millside Division. The final answering grunt on the line made it plain his second-in-command's enthusiasm was at a winter low – and the grunt changed to an incoherent splutter as Thane told him what they'd drawn. It needed little imagination to realize that Moss rated Braedale as one stage short of the North Pole.

Things were shaping into one of those days. And the promised beer and sandwiches with Buddha Ilford did little to improve the outlook. The C.I.D. boss spent most of the time complaining at the general iniquities of income tax and the particular injustices involved in what he had to pay. After which, he sat back and made a painfully slow show of fumbling for his money while Thane settled the bill.

Which still left Mary. He walked back to Headquarters with Ilford, left him there, and had the duty car run him home.

The sun was out, afternoon-low in the sky but bright. On an impulse he had the car stop at the end of his narrow street of small, egg-box identical bungalows, thanked the driver, and walked the rest of the way. Going along, he noted one consolation about winter. An the gardens looked pretty unkempt, his own front lot for once blended in with the rest.

He reached the path and swung in. All right, the house was small, but he liked it. Another ten years of mortgage repayments and they'd own the place. He chuckled wryly at the thought, decided that day would be worth a celebration, and was reaching for his key when the door opened.

14

'I saw you coming.' Mary Thane eyed him quizzically. 'How was the meeting?'

'All right,' he said lamely, giving her a brief, light kiss as they went in. 'But . . .'

'But you're not stopping.' She was dark-haired, petite, with a smooth, fresh complexion and a figure which seemed wrong for a woman with two school-age children. She nodded calmly. 'I heard. There's coffee ready and your bag's packed. I put in an extra sweater. It'll be cold up north.'

'Bush telegraph busy again?' He grimaced. Millside Division's switchboard girls and C.I.D. wives had an unwritten understanding which no man with any sense would attempt to challenge. 'Well, they're right as usual.'

'As usual.' A twinkle gathered in her eyes. 'Anyway, I'd have guessed. I'm only kissed on arrival when something's wrong.'

Thane decided that one was best left unanswered, hung up his coat, and followed her through to the lounge.

'It shouldn't be more than two or three days,' he said defensively, lowering himself into an armchair.

'Let's hope not.' She poured the coffee, stirred in his usual three spoonfuls of sugar, and brought the cup over. 'Otherwise there's going to be trouble when it comes to Monday night.'

He drank the coffee, the fact connecting. Monday was school concert night. Tommy had a fancy dress chorus role, Kate ranked as second assistant fairy in the grand finale.

'I'll make it,' he said quickly. The clock showed school was long since out but the house was oddly quiet. 'Where are they anyway?'

'They dumped their books and took Clyde for a walk. That dog needs more exercise – like some other people around here.' She ignored his mutter of protest and became more business-like. 'When *do* you have to leave?'

15

'Not for a while.' He laid the coffee cup on the floor, reached out, and suddenly hauled her on to his lap. 'So . . .'

She sighed in mock despair, wriggled into a more comfortable position, and put her arms around his neck.

A couple of minutes later, just as he was ready to suggest there were better places than a chair, the door burst open. Rocketing into the room, Clyde made a scrabbling, muddy-pawed attempt to climb up between them. Two small figures appeared in the doorway, stopped, and considered them suspiciously.

'We're back,' said Tommy.

'And we're hungry.' His sister eyed them with a frown. 'Is something wrong with mum?'

'No.' Thane smiled weakly. 'She's fine.'

'Then what are you doing to her?'

'Nothing.' It came ruefully. 'Not now, anyway.'

The Tom and Jerry show was getting under way on TV when the Headquarters car arrived at five-thirty. That meant Mary was the only one who bothered to see him off. She waved again from the porch as he heaved his bag into the back of the Jaguar, then he'd climbed aboard and had closed the door.

'Inspector Moss next, sir?' The driver waited for his nod then slipped the car into gear. As they pulled away the man spoke again. 'There's a package on the seat, Mr Thane. Chief Superintendent Ilford said to tell you he hoped it would be useful.'

Thane sat back, took the package, and stripped off the brown paper wrapping while the car travelled on. There was a book inside. He read the title and swore. *A Child's Guide to Farm Animals*. Ilford's humour was bent as a corkscrew.

Phil Moss didn't keep them waiting. As the car reached the old two-storey boarding house he called home, his thin, shabby figure came hurrying out to the pavement. He

16

came aboard with an ancient leather case clutched in one hand and a paper carrier bag shielded in the other.

As he lowered them and clawed the car door shut again the carrier bag clinked. Thane raised an eyebrow.

'Just a thing or two I might need,' said Moss reluctantly. A small, lean-faced bachelor with sparse sandy hair, he sniffed hard as the car began gathering speed through the dusk. 'It can pay to be prepared – doctors are scarce up north.'

'But you can always find a vet. In fact it might be an idea with your history,' murmured Thane. He leaned over, flicked open the top of the carrier bag and saw the loosely packed assortment of medicine bottles and pill boxes. 'Sure you didn't forget anything?'

Moss scowled as he heard what sounded like a chuckle coming from their driver and stayed perched on the edge of the seat. 'How long till we get to this place?' he demanded.

'About three hours' driving time,' said Thane unperturbed. 'But we'll stop and eat on the way.'

'And I can imagine what that'll mean,' said Moss greyly.

Thane chuckled. Moss and his stomach ulcer just had to be taken as they came. They constituted a part of Millside Division lore – and though Moss knew it, he didn't care. That ulcer was the daily barometer of his outlook, a considerable part of his existence seemed devoted to catering for its needs in any way possible that would shield it from the threat of a surgeon's knife.

Even without it, Moss was an unusual kind of cop. Aged vaguely in his mid-fifties, suit invariably baggy and shoes in need of repair, he had all the appearance of an overworked, grossly underpaid office clerk.

Which was where a lot of people made a mistake.

There was a lot more to Detective Inspector Phil Moss than a down-at-heel air and a dyspeptic view of humanity. And an underlying friendship built on established trust

17

was only a beginning of the reasons why Colin Thane frequently blessed the day they'd first been teamed to run Millside Division.

Thane brought out his cigarettes, passed one to the driver, gave another to Moss, and they smoked in silence for a spell. Gradually the city's lights began to fade behind them. Then, as the Jaguar reached the start of the broad A80 expressway north, Moss stirred again.

'You didn't tell me much in that call,' he complained.

'You didn't want to know much,' reminded Thane dryly. He went through the story again then nodded towards his overnight bag. 'The detail stuff we've got is in the file, but there's not much of it. It comes down to the fact that Fenn is an old-style cop. If someone needs their backside kicked he kicks.'

'Today's surest way of ending up on an assault charge,' commented Moss acidly. 'That's why he was banished to Braedale?'

'And lucky to stop there,' nodded Thane. 'The last backside he kicked had a good lawyer. But this time he's in real trouble. If he did kill this damned bull he could end up in jail for a couple of years at a minimum – and face civil action for damages on top of it.'

Moss gave an unusually sympathetic whistle. 'For fifty thousand quid on a cop's pay? He couldn't live that long.'

Engine note subtly changing, the Jaguar edged into the outer fast lane. An XJ6 model with a six cylinder 4.2 litre power unit, it had twin carburettors plus a siamesed exhaust and was one of the Headquarters transport pool's latest acquisitions. They'd done a little breathing work around the cylinder head and engine ports since it arrived. The output available was considerably above the regular 245 b.h.p. – and this was the first time there had been a genuine chance to try the result.

Foot gradually shading down on the accelerator, the driver hummed under his breath as his charge began to surge forward. Her headlamps lanced into a night which had become a rushing funnel, the speedometer swung up to pass the '100' mark.

Still the man hummed happily. Watching, frozen speechless for a spell, Moss swallowed each time tail lights glowed ahead in the liquid darkness. But traffic was minimal, any vehicles ahead took one rear-view mirror glance at what was coming and moved smartly into the middle lane. He took a deep breath and tried to sound nonchalant.

'What do we know about Jennings?' he asked. 'You said he was one of the Home Rule brigade. But what else?'

'He seems to be the "act don't talk about it" type.' Thane stubbed his cigarette in the rear seat ashtray keeping his eyes firmly away from the speedometer needle. 'In his own way Adam Jennings seems pretty much a parallel with Fenn. He worried the regular Nationalist Party branch so much they finally kicked him out a couple of years back. So now he runs his own little ginger group – the Children of the Mist.'

'Sounds like a bunch of beards and mini-skirts.'

'A lot of them are. But the file says Jennings has quite a few adult-style enthusiasts, the kind with money who're looking for excitement.'

'Excitement?' Moss snarled the word. 'They could always try being driven by some of the madmen working out of Headquarters.' Up front their driver winced and sadly eased his foot from the pedal. 'And Fenn's daughter – what's she like?'

'Sylvia Fenn, aged eighteen.' Thane shrugged. 'Seems she has the notion that Adam Jennings is the greatest thing since the Beatles.'

'Bright-eyed teenagers!' Moss belched his disgust and felt better for it. 'Well, maybe Jennings was playing around with her after hours and father found out.'

Thane shook his head. The file was blank on that aspect and on a lot of others. But the mental picture he'd formed of Fenn didn't fit the idea. If anything like Moss's suggestion had been going on he'd a feeling the County man would have been more likely to shoot Jennings than take it out on a prize bull.

The road narrowed and a small cluster of street lamps glinted ahead, the village of Bannockburn. To the left a bright white glow in the sky marked the site of the giant equestrian statue of Robert the Bruce – the Scots king who had long ago carved his way to immortality with a battle-axe, crushing an English army in the process.

That had been over 650 years back. Yet Bannockburn still rated as a national shrine, maybe more now than ever before.

The car purred on. A new, greater gathering of lights ahead marked Stirling town and its ancient hill-top castle – almost as precious in Scotland's history.

Colin Thane sat back and rubbed a hand across his chin, considering it all. Plenty of Scots sympathized with the active Nationalist minority. Plenty even voted that way, from a mixture of motives. Scotland might have gone in voluntary merger as far back as 1603 when England's virgin Queen Elizabeth died and a pimple-faced James VI of Scotland headed south to inherit her throne, the start of a newly United Kingdom. But the Scots had never really ceased to be a nation, independent, stubborn, cherishing their past, bleakly angry at being ignored by successive London-based governments.

Should it be status quo, federal rule, complete independence? A lot of voters would have thought it a big step forward if the average Westminster politician had been able to identify Scotland on a map.

His own view? He grinned in the darkness of the car, remembering his father – who'd been independent and stubborn in a lot of ways. His theory had been quite simply that no true Scot should feel an Englishman was an inferior. He should merely sympathize with him for being born in the wrong country.

Scot Nats? He'd met all kinds. From sturdy individuals with a hazy, half-planned dream, to wild men who'd gamble most things for their goal.

Adam Jennings seemed inclined towards the latter. But they weren't on their way to investigate Jennings. What mattered was a dead bull named Marquis – and a cop whose whole future was at stake.

There was a pretty horrible pun there. The kind that was best forgotten. He settled back and tried to ignore it.

Chapter Two

On the map, Glasgow to Braedale was a distance of 120 miles. They stopped roughly halfway to eat at a roadside inn, then were off again – but at a slower pace.

The main trunk routes were left behind. The remaining distance lay over roads which were narrow, winding, and little better than country lanes. The kind where only a fool cornered fast.

And was likely to end up a dead fool if he did.

Time crept on. Thane's wrist watch read close to 9.30 p.m. before the Jaguar's headlamps at last picked up the marker sign they wanted.

'Welcome to Braedale. Home of Fine Cattle.'

The words framed the black-on-white silhouette of an Angus bull's distinctive, polled head. But on the stone wall below someone had crudely aerosol-painted a postscript.

'Free Scotland Now. End English Dominasion.'

'Damn fools,' muttered Moss indignantly. 'Couldn't they have got the spelling right?'

Round another bend and beyond a clump of trees a narrow, hump-backed bridge took them over a rushing burn. Another minute, and they were in sight of Braedale village.

The cloud-wisped moonlight showed small, neat houses grouped round three sides of an open space which had once been a village green. Shops and other buildings formed the fourth side and most of the centre area held an assortment of parked cars and trucks.

'Over there.' Leaning forward, Thane pointed. 'The Clachan Arms. That's where Buddha said we'd be booked in.'

A neon hotel sign burned outside a white two-storey building. Nearer to them, people were streaming from the brightly lit open doors of what looked like the village hall. Some were already crossing towards the car park, others formed a crowd on the roadway.

'Some kind of meeting ended.' Moss frowned as the Jaguar slowed to a crawl. 'Give them a hoot. That'll move them.'

The driver thumbed his horn button. For a moment their way began to clear. Then, as the police uniform in front was spotted, a ragged cheer went up. Figures trotted alongside while the car nosed through towards the hotel. When it stopped, the cheer changed to noisy jeering.

Bewildered, their driver jerked on the handbrake and glanced round. 'Want me to sort them out, sir?'

'Relax, man,' said Thane with a touch of amusement. 'Take another look. They're mostly kids.'

Youngsters, anyway. Farming-style teenagers – which, from the press of bodies around, meant the mini-skirts were even shorter and the boys hairier than their city equivalents.

Grinning faces began to peer through the window glass. A few bold spirits banged their fists on the car roof.

'Do we wait until they turn us over?' queried Moss with an acid calm. 'If this is a Highland welcome you can keep it.'

Thane reached for the door handle, shoved it open against the crush, and heard a fresh mocking cheer as he started to climb out. There were between fifty and sixty in the crowd and suddenly their attention had a new objective as a tall, broad-shouldered figure appeared from the hall.

The noise grew, and the newcomer laughed, a wave of his arm enough to move any of the youngsters from his path. The lights gleamed on a mane of black wavy hair. He wore a thick tweed suit over an open-necked shirt.

'Get off home now, the lot of you!' The rich, deep voice boomed the words cheerfully as he reached Thane's side. 'Away, I tell you. What way is this to treat visitors?'

The crowd edged back, leaving a clear space around. The new arrival chuckled and turned apologetically to Thane.

'Don't worry about them. They don't mean any harm.'

'That's what I hoped,' grimaced Thane. 'What's going on?'

'Our weekly meeting. It was a good one too.' The man broke off, swung round again, and shouted above the din. 'Where's John MacGhee? Come on now, let him through, my Children!'

'He's on his way, Adam,' yelled someone from the edge of the circle.

The man acknowledged with a wave and watched with amusement as Moss cautiously emerged from the car.

'I didn't expect to meet you till tomorrow,' the deep voice said with a quiet amusement. 'Still sooner the better. I'm Adam Jennings. Which of you is Chief Inspector Thane?'

'I am.' Thane looked at the man with a new interest. Adam Jennings topped him by a couple of inches in height. The face was strong and bold-nosed, the grin showed white, regular teeth. This was a man it was easy to understand as a leader – a leader plenty would follow regardless of age. 'You knew we were coming?'

'I'd a phone call from County Headquarters.' Jennings beckoned as a short, bulky man wearing an open raincoat over a kilt and sporran broke through the encircling youngsters. 'John, can you take over? I've got to get home.'

'I'll move them,' said the newcomer confidently, a frown on his fleshy red face. He was middle-aged, the voice sharp and clipped. 'This is damned stupid.'

24

'High spirits,' murmured Jennings. He turned to Thane again. 'John MacGhee will look after you . . .'

'We don't exactly need an escort,' said Thane mildly.

'No, that's true.' Jennings smiled again. 'I'll have to go. I'm expecting a visitor. But you'll be round tomorrow?'

Thane nodded. Adam Jennings strode off, the crowd parting in the same magical way to let him through, more cheers ringing out.

'Well now –' John MacGhee cleared his throat impatiently – 'let's move out of this, eh?'

'That's the best idea yet,' grunted Moss. 'I'll get our stuff, Colin.'

The sight of their overnight bags brought new shouts from the crowd. Then, suddenly, the jeers switched to a gathering chant.

'Who killed the Marquis? Fenn . . . Fenn . . .' It grew to a roar. 'Who killed the Marquis? Fenn . . . Fenn . . . Fenn . . .'

MacGhee spun round, his kilt swinging.

'Adam told you to go home,' he bellowed. 'And cut that out!'

The chorus died and he shook his head. 'You can guess what that's about, I suppose. Still, if it's not too late, welcome to Braedale.'

'A quiet little place,' murmured Thane dryly. 'Well, we're ready.'

MacGhee nodded then looked past them, his mouth tightening. 'Damn the luck. Why did he have to turn up now?'

The uniformed police sergeant boring his way through towards them was thin and angry-looking. As he broke through, he grated a loud, bitter warning.

'Move, or I'll arrest the whole heathen lot of you.'

There was a roar of cynical laughter. Then, piercing above the din, a girl's voice sounded high and clear.

'Children of the Mist . . .'

The noise died. For a few brief seconds there was a total,

eerie silence. When it came, the response blended into a skin-prickling almost ritual cadenza from every throat.

'Free . . . dom. Free . . . dom.'

Shaking his head, the sergeant reached them.

'Sorry about this, sir.' He spoke instinctively to Thane. 'I'm Sergeant Imrie from Braedale Station. I got down as soon as I heard.'

'Let them have their fun.' Thane hoped it sounded convincing, listening as the chant began again. The fervour in those young voices held its own message for anyone who cared to listen. A message which he found difficult to ignore. 'I don't mind.'

'Aye, but plenty of people will,' said Imrie doggedly.

'Plenty?' John MacGhee was scornful. 'Only a few. Anyway, they're breaking up now. Cool down, sergeant.'

He was right. The crowd around was thinning, beginning to drift away, still occasionally sounding their chorus as they left.

'It's over,' said MacGhee. His fat face grinned in Thane's direction. 'And you don't need me now the sergeant has arrived. Not tonight anyway. But I imagine I'm on tomorrow's list – try and make it before 10 a.m., will you?'

Before any of them could answer he was heading away, the kilt swaying in tune with his heavy hips.

Thane shrugged, remembered their driver, and signalled he could leave. The Jaguar started up with a soft burble of exhaust and eased out from the kerb.

As its tail lights faded, heading back along the road to the south, Sergeant Imrie led his visitors through the glass door of the Clachan Arms Hotel. The elderly clerk behind the reception desk in the small, brightly lit lobby smoothed his jacket lapels as they came over.

'Things were noisy tonight, sergeant,' he complained. 'Are they finished now?'

'For another week,' agreed Imrie shortly. 'I'll talk about it later.'

26

'Aye.' The clerk said it in a hurt voice and pushed the register across his desk. 'Your rooms are ready, gentlemen. Eight and nine, upstairs.'

They signed the book then followed the clerk up the stairway with Imrie bringing up the rear. The rooms were small, plainly furnished, considerably colder than the lobby area, but scrupulously clean.

Imrie hovered in the background until the clerk had plodded back towards his post. Then, standing in the open doorway of Thane's room, he cleared his throat in loud, hopeful fashion.

'About tomorrow, sir. Will nine o'clock be early enough? I can make it earlier . . .'

'The time's all right.' Thane lowered his bag on to the bed and came over slowly, his face expressionless. 'But I'm not so sure about you, sergeant. I've a file which says it was a Sergeant Imrie who reported he'd seen Inspector Fenn's car near the Jennings farm. Right?'

'Yes.' The answer came reluctantly.

'And there's only one Sergeant Imrie in Braedale?'

'Aye.' The man's mouth tightened. 'Only one, sir. But Charlie Fenn's a good cop, whatever he may have done – if he's done anything. And Adam Jennings is . . .'

'We've met Jennings,' snapped Thane, cutting him short. 'Right now I'm more interested in you, sergeant. It wouldn't take too much imagination to guess you could have reached us earlier outside. That you wanted us to have a little taste of the Children of the Mist as a starter to this job.'

Imrie met his gaze, swallowed, but said nothing. Appearing behind him, Phil Moss edged forward into the room.

'Let's get this straight.' Moss's thin, sharp features frowned at the man. 'Sergeant, who assigned you to be our attached liaison man? Did the order come from Head-quarters – or from Inspector Fenn?'

'Neither. Headquarters just said to arrange it. With the

27

inspector suspended, I'm in charge.' Imrie eyed them uneasily, his voice became a low mutter. 'Ach, it was my own idea. And why not?'

'Imrie, you're either a fool or plain thick-headed.' Thane glared at the man. 'You're a major witness in this mess, if you'd some crazy idea of helping Fenn you couldn't have come up with a worse one. And if your name hadn't been on that file . . .' He sighed despairingly and left the rest unsaid. 'Sergeant, you'll assign another man for tomorrow. We'll forget the rest. Understood?'

'Yes, sir.' Imrie flushed and made to leave.

'Hold on.' Thane beckoned him back. 'What did MacGhee mean outside when he said he'd expect us tomorrow?'

'That?' The County man gave a shrug. 'I thought you'd know. He's the local vet – the one who did the post mortem on the bull.'

'And his connection with the Children of the Mist?'

'Adam Jennings' private army, you mean,' retorted Imrie grimly. 'He's got some title like assistant secretary. The kilt is part of the act.'

'You don't like MacGhee?'

'I didn't know I had to like either of them . . . sir.' There was just enough of a pause between the words to hold its own brand of defiance.

Thane let him go. As he stalked off towards the stairs Phil Moss chuckled softly.

'That put some salt on his tail.'

'For now. But he'll need watching.' Thane stretched wearily and yawned. 'Let's go down and have a beer. Then I'm for bed. I'm getting a feeling that tomorrow could be one of those long, long days.'

'They usually are,' said Moss pointedly. 'Give me a moment then I'm ready.'

He went back to his room. There was a rustle of paper then a clink of glass. Curiosity roused, Colin Thane crossed to the open doorway and looked in.

A small bottle in one hand, a spoon in the other, Moss was pouring a careful measure of pale amber liquid. Satisfied, he swallowed the dose at a gulp, grimaced, then saw Thane as he recorked the bottle.

'Olive oil,' he explained earnestly. 'Keeps the stomach walls lubricated – well, gives a sort of protective coating. It's good for anyone. Like some?'

Thane shuddered and thumbed towards the stairs.

The hotel bar was long, narrow and moderately busy. Grey stone walls were decorated with framed photographs of massive Black Angus cattle, the rest was furnished plainly. The obvious aim was to cater for serious drinking as distinct from social loitering.

Yet the customers didn't completely fit. Only one small group were middle-aged, tweedy, and as agricultural as the mud on their heavy brown boots. They were a slightly uncomfortable minority among the cheerfully noisy parties of casually dressed youngsters.

Standing inside the doorway, Moss nudged as one of the farmers paid for a new round of drinks. The money was peeled casually from a crumpled, fist-thick wad of notes.

'Practically throwing the stuff around,' he muttered. 'I thought farmers were always on the breadline.'

'Up here they call it the cakeline,' Thane corrected. 'Forget about them. Keep an eye on the rest. It looks like some of the Children are in for a late-night dew.'

The farmer went back to his friends. Thane headed for the gap at the bar counter and ordered. The barmaid, a stout, tight-mouthed brunette, poured their drinks in a disinterested silence then reached for the coins he slid across the counter.

A thin bronzed hand beat her to it, pushed Thane's money aside, and waved a pound note under her nose.

'I'm paying, Maggie.' The owner, a tall, gangling young man with red hair and wearing a blue rally jacket, gave

29

Thane an easy grin. 'Call it a peace offering. The lads maybe overdid things a bit outside.'

'You didn't approve?' The pound had been taken, the change was already going back into the redhead's pocket.

'I didn't say that, Chief Inspector.' The grin remained. 'You'll drink with us?'

The noise along the bar had faded. Conscious of his audience, Thane lifted his glass and looked around at the waiting faces. A girl giggled and was frowned to silence by her companions.

'To everyone,' he said mildly, and sipped.

The faces relaxed, conversations picked up again. Sniffing a little, Phil Moss picked up the other glass and turned to the redhead.

'You seem to know why we're here,' he said flatly.

'Everybody does.' The redhead's voice became earnest, rising. 'Up here plenty of people have a feud going with their neighbours. It rates near enough to a local pastime. But your Inspector Fenn went away over the odds – hell, killing a beast like the Marquis rates worse than murder.'

'If he did it, you mean,' corrected Thane.

'Adam Jennings says he did.' The reply came loudly from a chunkily built figure in jeans and heavy sweater. 'That's good enough for us.'

His friends muttered agreement. In the background, the older drinkers stayed quiet.

'For you, maybe. Not for us,' said Thane flatly. He turned to the redhead again, speaking softly. 'Still, that doesn't mean we're not ready to listen. You know Fenn's daughter?'

'Sylvia?' He nodded. 'She's a nice kid, not like her old man. And if you want to hear more, the name's Dave Anderson. I work at the garage across the square.'

'We'll be around.' Thane glanced along the bar. 'You've plenty of friends in here.'

Anderson's grin returned. 'Only because this is Wednesday – market day. Most of the farmers are doing their drinking down in Perth tonight, so we can move in. Other nights –' he shook his head – 'well, not everyone likes the Children of the Mist. Not in quantity, anyway.'

'That's maybe understandable,' said Moss with a frosty edge. He nodded past the redhead. 'How many of you carry those things?'

A half-dozen of the Children were sitting round the nearest table, talking and drinking. The nearest had one leg hooked around his chair, showing a clear gap of leg between sock-top and trouser cuff . . . with a small black knife-hilt protruding from the sock-top.

'That?' Anderson laughed at Moss's frown, reached down to his own sock-top, and brought out an identical knife. Sliding it into the palm of his hand, he held it out for inspection. 'Would that harm anyone?'

The short, three-inch hilt was of plain bone. The blade, roughly the same length, was in cheap, soft steel, moderately sharp but with a carefully rounded point.

'Charlie Fenn tried to cause trouble about them,' mused Anderson. 'That's why we had the points rounded off – they're issued that way now.'

'Issued?' Thane raised an eyebrow. 'You mean it's some kind of membership badge?'

Anderson nodded. 'For committee members. The rest have a lapel pin.'

Thane took the knife, balanced it for a moment, then handed it back. 'There was a committee meeting going on when the Marquis was shot.'

'Social sub-committee,' agreed Anderson. 'None of us heard anything.' He slid the knife back into its sock-sheath. 'If we had, we might have caught him then and there. And saved you a lot of trouble, eh?'

'Maybe.'

'You mean . . .' Anderson stopped, shook his head, and

31

chuckled. 'Citizen's arrest, that's what I had in mind. Nothing more – I'm the peaceful type.'

He gave a vague mock salute and strolled back to his friends.

Thane and Moss finished their beers, followed them with a whisky each, and talked for a little while the bar gradually emptied. Then Thane caught himself yawning. That 3 a.m. call and the late Harry-Boy Tait were catching up on him.

Moss yawned in turn and blew his nose on an off-white handkerchief. 'Too much damned fresh air, that's what's wrong,' he declared.

They emptied their glasses and left the bar as the farmers began calling for another round.

By the time Thane was in his pyjamas and between the sheets his eyelids were beginning to gum down. He lay back, trying to plan out the day ahead. But it was too much of an effort. His mind kept drifting back to Adam Jennings – the way that black-haired, confident giant had shown such complete, fully accepted control over his Children.

That wasn't going to help.

He reached for the light switch. Then tensed as a strange, animal-like moaning began somewhere near. It started low, but grew fast to a note one stage short of agony.

The climax was a splutter and a familiar, muffled belch.

Phil Moss was having his late-night gargle. And the walls of the Clachan Arms were far from soundproof.

Sighing, Thane switched off the light, sagged back, and fell asleep.

Morning arrived in the shape of an elderly, brisk-voiced chambermaid who hammered on the room door as she came in. She declared it was raining and thumped a cup of lukewarm tea by the bedside as she turned to leave.

32

Shaved and dressed, Colin Thane went down to the dining room at eight-thirty. He found Moss already there, installed at a corner table by the window. Outside the early morning darkness was already busy. Vehicles rumbled past and pools of light showed the village shops were open for business.

Thane ordered bacon and eggs from a grey-faced waiter who looked like he was nursing a hangover. When the order came Thane nodded his thanks then gestured at the empty tables all around.

'Where's everybody?'

The waiter shrugged. 'We're quiet this time of year. We've only yourselves and another fellow booked in.'

He shuffled off in a way which made it clear that was a total of three too many.

They were still eating when the door swung open and a tall young figure in police uniform looked in. He saw them, came straight over, and snapped a salute at Moss.

'Constable Copeland, sir.' The shoulders were stiff. 'Reporting as ordered.'

'Tell him.' Moss used his fork to point across the table.

Copeland, muscular in build and with a broken nose, swung round. His face reddened. 'Sorry, sir. Reporting as . . .'

'Ordered,' agreed Thane with a touch of sympathy. He nodded towards a vacant chair. 'There's no hurry.'

Copeland lowered himself carefully and placed his peaked cap on one knee.

'Well, you know why we're here.' Thane pushed his plate aside and lit a cigarette. 'You haven't been involved yet?'

'No, sir.' Copeland shook his head quickly. 'I only got back from leave yesterday. That's why I got – uh . . .'

'Landed with us?' queried Moss innocently.

Thane ignored him. 'We've to see the vet before ten. How about Adam Jennings and his cattleman?'

33

'They're usually out in the fields till about noon, sir.'

'Then they can wait.' Thane tried to keep his manner every-day. 'Where's the – ah – body?'

'Next door to here, sir.' Copeland saw their eyebrows rising and explained hastily. 'It was a bit of a problem what to do with a thing that size, but we managed to make a deal with Allison the Butcher. We're using part of his cold store. For a few days anyway.'

Thane nodded. 'All right, we'll have a look.'

'You mean both of us?' Moss gave the idea no particular welcome. He muttered on under his breath, one stage short of rebellion. 'I don't mind taking Copeland's word on it. Or do you think it has got up and walked off?'

'Both of us,' said Thane firmly. 'That's why we're here.' He turned to Copeland again. 'While we're doing that, get hold of Sergeant Imrie and tell him we'll want to talk later. He can pass the same word to Inspector Fenn.'

'Yes, sir.' Copeland hesitated. 'There was a wee spot of trouble at Inspector Fenn's home last night, late on. Some drunk smashed one of the front windows with a brick.'

'And got away?'

The constable nodded ruefully. 'More's the pity.'

Thane considered him for a minute. 'You're on Fenn's side?'

'Yes.' Copeland flushed. 'But I'll do my job.' He shoved back his chair and rose. 'I'll have the car waiting when you're ready, sir.'

He left them. Moss gave a lop-sided grin as the door swung shut again.

'Another member of the Charlie Fenn Fan Club.' He stifled a yawn. 'Well, let's go and see the Marquis. Might as well get it over with.'

Thane nodded and stubbed his cigarette.

Inspector Fenn certainly seemed to foster a strong brand of loyalty. The kind that wouldn't make their job any easier.

*   *   *

34

Allison the Butcher was a stumpy little barrel of a man with a blue and white striped apron, a fluffy tonsure of hair and a small red nose. His shop was crowded. But he abandoned the waiting customers and proudly led his visitors past the dangling legs of beef and sides of lamb in the back shop and out a small door into an outside yard.

'In here.' He stopped at a large brick-built shed, fumbled under his apron for the key, and unlocked the metal double doors. 'And though I say it, there's not a better cold store this side o' Perth.'

They waited patiently in the grey, pre-dawn drizzle while he put the key away again and tugged one door open.

'In we go.' Beckoning cheerfully, Allison led the way. Inside, the temperature hit them like a freezing wall. Shivering, they looked around as a neon tube light sputtered to life. Most of the store's space was filled by hanging carcases of meat. But an area had been cleared to one side and a tarpaulin-wrapped bundle lay against the wall. Allison went over, seized a corner of the tarpaulin, and brought it back with a flourish.

'There's a bonnie beast, eh?'

Like some black mountain, a mountain now covered by a delicate white powdering of frost, the Marquis of Braedale lay stretched before them. Lifeless eyes stared vacantly. The small, neat mouth lay open and a grey-blue tongue protruded. But it was the sheer size and perfectly formed shape of the dead bull which held them momentarily hypnotized.

Even in death the Marquis retained an aristocratic air. This had certainly been no ordinary animal.

'Aye, a bonnie young beast,' mused Allison. 'Now you'll want to see what happened.'

The small round hole was through the forehead, between and just above the eyes. A thin fringe of singed hair and powder-burned skin showed the shot had been fired at close range.

'That's all?' queried Moss.

'It was enough.' Allison rubbed his hands together for warmth. 'One shot, right into the brain. A professional slaughterman couldn't have done better.'

They'd seen enough. Slightly disappointed, the man replaced the tarpaulin and followed them back out into the drizzling rain.

'How'd you get the body moved here?' asked Thane.

'With a breakdown truck an' a crane.' Allison looked at them hopefully. 'You'll be finished in another day or two, eh? If you are, I can maybe still do something wi' the carcase – locally, I mean.'

Still shivering, Phil Moss made a tooth-sucking sound of disgust. Thane edged him aside.

'We'll try,' he promised smoothly.

How the County Medical Officer or the area Food Hygiene inspector would have reacted to that was a different matter. He could sort it out later, make a phone call to someone.

But not yet.

Quarrel with Allison and a problem could be dumped on their laps. A half-ton problem.

The rain was easing and after the bone-chilling temperature of the cold store the walk back to the Clachan Arms was welcome exercise. They found Constable Copeland sheltering in the hotel doorway then exchanged glances as they saw the car. It was a small white beat-patrol Austin Mini.

'We're low on transport, sir,' said Copeland apologetically. 'Sergeant Imrie said it would have to do.'

'It will,' sighed Thane. He guessed Imrie had gained a slice of satisfaction out of this one. Once Moss had shoe-horned into the rear seat he climbed in at the front beside Copeland and they set off.

Swinging round the village square, Copeland suddenly grinned as they passed a small garage. He gave a touch on the horn button. Two figures were standing beside the brightly lit pumps. One was Dave Anderson, in mechanic's overalls. The other was a girl, long dark hair hiding most of her face, her hands deep in the pockets of a short-length raincoat.

Anderson waved a greeting. The girl gave the car a glance then turned away.

'Inspector Fenn's daughter,' said Copeland shortly. 'Things must be a bit difficult for her.'

'Oh?' Moss peered back through the rear window. 'Meaning she doesn't know whose side she's on?'

Copeland shrugged and said nothing.

A ten-minute drive through the dawn light brought them to John MacGhee's home. The veterinary surgeon lived in a compact modern bungalow set a little way back from the road, a radio transmitter mast rising high beside it. They turned off and stopped on a tarmac driveway beside a parked, empty Land-Rover.

As Copeland made to get out Thane stopped him.

'Better stay. We won't be long.'

Copeland looked far from pleased but nodded. They left him, walked over to the house, and rang the doorbell. To one side a brass plate advised that John MacGhee, M.R.C.V.S., held surgery consultations between 8 and 10 a.m. on weekdays.

After a moment the door opened and a woman in a white overall coat greeted them with a smile.

'Mr Thane?'

He nodded. 'And Inspector Moss.'

She was middle-aged, neatly built and with a friendly face. Her hair was dark with a few traces of grey, back-combed and softly waved.

'You're expected. I'm Margaret Linton, Mr MacGhee's assistant.'

37

They went into a linoleum-tiled waiting-room area. There was a wooden bench along one wall and a faint smell of disinfectant in the air. The woman knocked on a frosted glass door marked 'Surgery', opened it, and gestured them through.

A pleased expression on his broad, fleshy face, John MacGhee rose from behind an old-fashioned desk as they entered. He was in a dark blue sports coat with grey corduroy slacks.

'You're in good time.' A large hand gestured towards the cup on his desk. 'How about some coffee?'

'Too soon after breakfast,' said Thane, shaking his head.

'Maybe, if you keep city hours.' MacGhee winked at the woman. 'How long have we been at it, Maggie?'

'Since before eight.' She gave him a wintry look. 'Will you want me?'

'Not for a spell. Keep an eye on the shop.' MacGhee waited till she'd gone then chuckled. 'My Miss Linton hates being called Maggie – which is why I do it.' He saw Thane eyeing his clothes and grinned. 'No kilt, eh? Sorry, but that's purely for ceremonials like last night's meeting. Adam Jennings likes a touch of the tartan among his platform party.'

'You feel differently?' Thane sat near the desk, which was littered with papers. Near it, a glass-fronted cabinet held an untidy assortment of instruments and equipment.

'The kilt is an abomination, Thane.' MacGhee's heavy shoulders shaped a shudder. 'Ever worn one?'

'Not for a long time,' admitted Thane. He'd been at school then, with no chance to refuse.

'Exactly!' MacGhee sniffed hard. 'Granted there's the old romantic thing about it. But our ancestors must have been damned hardy. It cuts the back of your knees in the wet and the draught in a wind will do anyone a guaranteed injury. Adam wants tartan on meeting nights and I oblige – but it amounts to a personal sacrifice.'

Moss had found a chair on the other side of the room. His notebook and pencil were ready beside him on a large rubber-topped examination table.

MacGhee hunched forward. 'Right, where do we start?'

'From when you were called out,' suggested Thane.

'That was 7 a.m.' MacGhee clipped his way through the sequence. 'Adam phoned and told me they'd just found the Marquis had been shot. I went straight over.'

'You live alone?' queried Moss from the background.

'Uh-huh. I've a wife somewhere but I haven't seen her in years.' MacGhee brushed the matter aside. 'Anyway, I got out to Broomvale Farm – Adam's place – before seven-thirty. I made a preliminary examination, of course. Reckoned time of death had been around 1 a.m. Which tied in.'

'Meaning?'

MacGhee blinked. 'Well, that was roughly when Fenn was seen prowling near the house by Tommy Dougan. Dougan is no fool. He happens to be Adam's head cattleman.'

'Dougan saw someone,' murmured Thane. 'But from what I heard he isn't sure. He only thinks it might have been Fenn.'

'Well, if you want to split hairs . . .' MacGhee shrugged his own view.

'Were you at the meeting at Broomvale that night?'

'No. Should have been, but I was too busy.' MacGhee clasped his hands. 'Let's see – yes. While I was deciding how to organize a post mortem Adam told me he'd bypassed the local station and had called County Head-quarters. Even so, it was still Sergeant Imrie who arrived first – but that wasn't my business. I did the p.m. in the afternoon. Once a beast is dead it goes to the end of the queue.' He pawed the papers on his desk and handed over a thin clip of close-typed sheets. 'Full autopsy report. Keep it – I had Maggie run off a few copies.'

'Thanks.' Thane folded the report and tucked it away. 'Like to boil it down for me?'

'That's simple enough.' MacGhee sat back. 'Cause of death was a .38 bullet fired at close range – something under eighteen inches, I'd guess. The bullet lodged in the brain and death was instantaneous. It was quite neatly done. A bull's brain is fairly small.'

'And the bullet?' queried Moss.

'I gave it to Sergeant Imrie. He was present and took some photographs before we started. And you'll see Maggie's signature is beside mine on the report. I had her along because it seemed the kind of job where her supporting evidence might prove useful.'

'Because of the insurance aspect?' murmured Thane.

'That?' MacGhee shook his head. 'They'll pay out all right – there's nothing else they can do. I meant because of Fenn.'

'There's still a lot of money involved,' prompted Thane.

'I know.' MacGhee grimaced. 'It's a mess, a real mess. Damn it, the Marquis was due to be shipped out to America next month and in a way I wasn't even looking forward to that.' He saw their faces and spread his hands apologetically. 'Well, I'd got to like the brute. I'd been seeing it two or three times a week for more than a month – the usual tests and checks before I could give a health certificate for export. That's one of my jobs around here. I'm a part-time Department of Agriculture local veterinary inspector. It's a fairly common arrangement.'

'Were there any problems about the certificate?'

'With the Marquis?' John MacGhee laughed aloud at the idea. 'None. But there's a standard isolation period before any export certificate is issued, and you keep tabs on the animal throughout.' He sighed. 'Make no mistake, Thane. From a vet's viewpoint attending the Marquis was almost a privilege – one I'm not likely to have again.'

'You mean Adam Jennings can't produce another like him?'

'Not in a dozen years. Hell, that's why the price was so high.' MacGhee didn't hide his disgust at their ignorance. 'That head, the line of body, the proportionate girth, colour, dressing percentage – the Marquis was unique. As a breed improver a bull like that could have been a real ambassador for Scotland.'

Spreading joy as he went. Keeping a suitably solemn face Thane nodded and rose. 'I'll keep in touch,' he promised. 'Phil . . .'

They said goodbye and left. Outside in the hall Margaret Linton was talking to a woman carrying a small, alarmingly pregnant dachshund. She left the woman and came over.

'You got all you wanted, Chief Inspector?'

'For now.' Thane glanced towards the dachshund. 'Business comes in all sizes?'

'Down to white mice,' she agreed, smiling. 'Small animals are my side of the practice – usually, anyway. John concentrates on the cattle and around here that's a big enough job on its own. In fact I'm as much secretary as assistant. Most of the day he's out around the farms. If an urgent call comes in I've the radio link to the Land-Rover – I can call and divert him.'

Phil Moss beat her to opening the front door. 'And you like the job, Miss Linton?'

'I've had worse.' The dachshund yelped behind them and she grimaced. 'Back to work.'

Outside, the sun had come up. As the door closed behind them Moss stood where he was, an odd expression on his face.

'Something wrong?' asked Thane, slowing.

'No. Nothing.' Moss shook his head quickly and hurried to join him. 'Well, where next? Is it still Sergeant Imrie and his sidekick?'

41

'Yes.' Thane glanced at him again, still puzzled. 'You're sure there's nothing wrong?'

'I said so, didn't I?' It came testily.

Thane shrugged and gave up. 'All right. But you take Imrie, Phil. I'm going to try Inspector Fenn on my own.'

'The personal touch?' Moss sniffed at the notion. 'And the best of luck – you'll probably need it.'

Chapter Three

The sky had cleared, the clouds had gone. As the Mini headed back towards the village the sun's rays glinted on a distant horizon of snow-capped mountains.

But the mountains were many miles away. Here the countryside was level, heavily wooded, but still predominantly grassland.

Cattle grazed in the rich, wet fields. They were sturdy cross-bred beef animals who looked up briefly with steam still rising from their short, hairy coats and vapour snorting from their nostrils. The prize Angus breeding stock were absent, most still snug in their farmyard winter quarters.

When a man's bank balance and future prosperity walked on four legs he took good care it came to no harm.

Or tried to.

Set on the north side of the village, Braedale police station was a long, single-storey brick building. As the car reached it and stopped Copeland pointed to a small bungalow further down the road.

'That's Inspector Fenn's house, sir.' He cleared his throat awkwardly. 'I'd – well, take it gently, sir. He can be pretty quick-tempered.'

'Which makes two of us,' Thane told him bluntly. 'Phil . . .'

'Uh?' Moss's mind had been far away.

'Tell Sergeant Imrie I want to know when Fenn last had

43

a routine police medical, and the details. County Head-quarters will have them.' He turned to Copeland again. 'Don't disappear. We'll need the car again.'

Leaving them, Thane walked down the road towards the house. As he got nearer and saw the smashed glass in one of the front windows his mouth tightened. Fenn wasn't having it easy. Not now.

A sheet of transparent plastic had been pinned behind the broken pane. It flapped gently in the light breeze as he went past the well-kept little garden and rapped the brass door-knocker. The door was opened by a burly man with iron grey hair and a neat, well-trimmed moustache.

'Chief Inspector Thane?' The man looked at him with bleak blue eyes. 'I'm Fenn. Come in.'

Thane stepped past him. Inspector Fenn's uniform jacket hung on one of a row of pegs in the tiny hallway, but he was in old khaki slacks and a faded yellow roll-neck jersey.

They went into the room with the shattered window. It had comfortable, old-fashioned furniture and a coal fire burned in the hearth. But a cold draught was coming round the edges of the plastic sheeting – and the temperature seemed to drop still lower as he saw who was waiting.

The girl he remembered from outside the garage. Face pale, she wore no make-up. Her eyes were red around the lids and swollen as if she'd been crying a lot and recently. But otherwise she was a pert-nosed, good-looking young-ster. The woman standing at her side was heavier in build and wore her dark hair cut short. But there was an unmis-takable facial resemblance.

'My daughter Sylvia, my wife Isobel.' Fenn made the introductions with a forced courtesy.

The girl tried to smile and failed. Her mother said noth-ing, her lips pressed tight in a tense, expectant line.

'Sylvia –' Fenn jerked his head towards the door – 'away to your room. Isobel, you'd better go too.'

44

The girl went quickly. Her mother didn't move.

'I'd rather stay,' she said bluntly.

'No need.' Fenn shook his head. Then his voice softened a little. 'Go on, lass. I'll manage – he's on his own.'

She hesitated, appeared ready to argue, then gave way under his steady gaze and followed her daughter. As the door closed, Fenn took a deep breath and turned to Thane again.

'Aye, you're on your own – this time.' One hand made a brief gesture of understanding. 'In your shoes, I'd probably do the same. For a start, anyway.'

'It seemed best.' Thane found the words awkward. 'If there is such a thing.'

'Meaning you don't like this any more than I do?' Fenn gave a humourless imitation of a laugh. 'Well, I'm under suspension. So I'm going to have a drink. Want one?'

'It would help,' nodded Thane.

Opening a cupboard, Fenn took out a bottle and two glasses, poured a generous measure of whisky into each, and handed one to Thane. 'Here . . . and this doesn't mean I'm hitting the stuff.' Glancing at the broken window, he added half to himself, 'Not that I don't feel like doing it.'

Thane sat on the nearest of the chairs. Charles Fenn . . . the file listed fifteen years' service, beginning as a beat cop. Before that, twelve years in the Army, where he'd made the rank of sergeant. He noted the framed wedding photograph on the sideboard. It had been an Army wedding. Beside the fireplace an old baton hung from a nail. That made him wince a little. He kept one there himself, just in case. Most cops did. Don't think of him as a cop, that was what Buddha Ilford had said. But it wasn't easy.

Fenn stabbed a sudden, impatient forefinger. 'Sergeant Imrie says he saw me driving from the Jennings place the night before last. You want to know if I admit that. Right?'

45

Thane nursed his glass. 'Yes. Particularly as Imrie seems to be on your side.'

'In a mess like this?' Fenn shook his head. 'Then he's a damned fool. But he's not blind. I was there. Around 1.20 a.m., in the clothes I'm wearing and in my own car.'

The admission came as a surprise. 'That's more than you told your Assistant Chief.'

'Old Windy Meikle?' Fenn grunted. 'Well, maybe I wasn't too clever there. But he rubbed me the wrong way. I was in no mood for his stand-at-attention stuff.'

'And now you're suspended.' Thane gave him no sympathy. 'There's another story – that you were seen prowling around Jennings' farmyard.'

'Was I?' Fenn took a long swallow from his glass. 'And I suppose your whiter-than-white Jennings also has a whole row of witnesses who saw me shoot his damned bull?'

'I haven't talked to him yet. I wanted your version first.' Thane eyed him calmly. 'Were you at the farmhouse?'

'Yes. And at 1 a.m.' Fenn snarled the words. 'Now you want to know why.' He scowled at the broken window. 'Well, I went there for a personal reason. I found I was – was mistaken about something and came away again. I didn't go near the animal pens and I didn't have a gun. Satisfied?'

'No, and you know I'm not.' Thane set down his glass and rose. 'Did you go there looking for your daughter?'

'My daughter was at home that night, all night.' Fenn's voice was hoarse, his face reddening as his finger stabbed again. 'Leave my family out of this, Thane. I've admitted being there – that's the beginning and the end of what you're getting.'

'All right.' Thane took out his cigarettes and lit one with deliberate care, giving the man time to come off the boil. Fenn was covering up on something, but covering up just how much and why? He tried again. 'With the kind of circumstantial evidence against you, you're really in trouble. So let's get down to basics. You've a reputation for disliking Jennings – which is putting it mildly. Why?'

'Because of what he's doing.' Fenn found his glass was empty, crossed to the cupboard, and refilled it. But he didn't drink. 'Most people laugh at this Children of the Mist thing he runs, think of it as a bit of nonsense.'

'You think differently?'

'I know differently,' grated Fenn. 'Jennings has half of those teenage kids and a good scattering of adults brain-washed into thinking anything is right if he says so. Any-thing.' He walked towards the fireplace then swung round. 'They're supposed to go to lectures on political history and hold tea-and-buns social raffles. What they do is hear him preach violence. Preach it and justify it – because he believes in it. And Thane, they're not just in Braedale. He has other Children of the Mist branches up and down Scotland. One day he's going to turn them loose – and they could cause havoc.'

'So you say he's more than a regular-grade fanatic,' mused Thane. He drew on his cigarette. 'Then why let your daughter stay one of the Children?'

Fenn hesitated then gave a helpless shrug. 'How the hell do I stop her? Lock the girl up and throw away the key? Damn it, I've done about everything else. Her mother's tried too. But she's been as stubborn, as – as . . .'

'As her father?' Abruptly, Thane switched to a new tack again. 'The file says you were Regular Army. What regiment?'

'Black Watch, the Royal Highlanders.' Fenn's eyes nar-rowed. 'What about it?'

'When you finished, did you bring any souvenirs home?'

'Like a .38 revolver?' Fenn took a deep breath. 'There's a .22 rifle in the garage. It's licensed and I use it for rabbits. That's the only gun I've got. There's no revolver, never has been. Look if you like.'

'Maybe we'll need to, later. But one way or another we'd

be wasting our time.' Thane threw his half-smoked cigarette into the fire. 'That's all for now. I'll be back.'

Fenn didn't move as he left the room. The lobby was empty. A sound like a muffled sob came from somewhere at the back of the house as Thane let himself out.

Passing the broken window he saw Charles Fenn still standing by the fireplace. The man's face was suddenly older, lined, very tired.

'There's nothing like patient perseverance when you come up against an idiot.' Leaning against a radiator, both hands wrapped round a mug of steaming tea, Detective Inspector Phil Moss delivered the acid pronouncement then added, 'Particularly when the idiot concerned happens to wear police uniform.'

The radiator was in one of the police station side rooms. Thane had found him there, with a worried, red-faced Sergeant Imrie standing opposite.

'Meaning?' Thane glanced sharply at Imrie. The man's flush deepened.

'Sergeant Imrie had forgotten something.' Moss shifted his stance to avoid being singed where it might hurt. 'At least let's say he'd forgotten. Otherwise he'd have mentioned a few extra facts in his report. Right, sergeant?'

'I suppose so.' Imrie gnawed his lip. 'But I still don't think . . .'

'Nobody wants you to think,' said Moss with a weary edge. 'Your memory has returned. That's enough for now.'

'Well, sergeant?' Thane waited, getting no hint from Moss's thin, sardonic features.

'Ach –' Imrie shrugged – 'it's only that Inspector Fenn would know we'd see him leaving Jennings' place. He'd ordered us to be watching the farm.'

'Ordered?' Thane rasped the word, the idea startling him with its possibilities.

'Yes, sir. The same as any other night when we heard

Jennings was to have one of his Children of the Mist committee meetings.' Imrie hesitated then decided the safest thing was to go straight on. 'There's a spot where we can hide the patrol car off the road and still see who comes and goes. We – well, we just watch and note any strange licence plates.'

'I see.' Thane struggled to keep his voice level. 'The first story was that you were on your way to a road accident. Mind explaining that, sergeant?'

'There was an accident, sir.' Imrie shuffled his feet uncomfortably. 'It was up on the Moortop Road. The call came over the radio just about the same time . . .'

'1.26 a.m.,' said Moss dryly. 'Five minutes after they saw Fenn go past. I checked the station logbook. That's what made me wonder. Somebody's timing had to be wrong otherwise the sergeant was on his way to an accident before anyone knew it had happened.'

'There was an accident all right,' protested Imrie. 'The car was wrecked – skidded on a corner an' hit a tree. The driver's in hospital with head injuries and a broken hip. He stunk of liquor.'

'And now there's another kind of smell around here,' muttered Moss.

Thane ignored the comment. 'All right, Imrie. You doctored that report. Why?'

Imrie moistened his lips. 'Because where Inspector Fenn had been didn't seem to matter – not until the morning, when we got word the Marquis had been shot dead. And –' he rubbed the palm of one hand nervously along the side of his tunic – 'well, the watch on Jennings' place is kind of unofficial. County Headquarters doesn't know about it.'

'That figures.' Thane dragged a chair over and sat down, feeling in need of support. 'How long has this been going on?'

'We only do it if we've heard there's to be a meeting at the farm, sir. And if anything else turned up . . .'

Thane cut him short with a glare. 'How long?'

Imrie swallowed hard. 'Three months, sir. Ever since there was that raid on the Army ammunition store over near Dunkeld.'

It rang a faint bell. Thane turned hopefully. 'Phil?'

'Perth County circulated the details,' nodded Moss. 'It was a straight break-in job. Some neds cut a hole in the barbed wire at the rear and sneaked past the sentries. The Army lost four cases of engineering demolition charges – nitrostarch, damned powerful stuff – and some acid-pencil detonator fuses.' He eased himself along the radiator again. 'The theory was that a bunch of city-style safe-blowers were stocking up for the winter season.'

'But Inspector Fenn had other ideas?' Thane eyed Imrie with a sardonic innocence. 'Surprise me. Tell me he blamed the Children of the Mist.'

Imrie nodded. 'He put the idea to Headquarters, but they didn't think much of it. And – well, he's in trouble enough. I thought if this special watch came out on top of the rest . . .'

'You thought . . .' Thane leaned his head on his hands. 'Sergeant, every time you think, you make matters worse. You're more than a problem. You're shaping into a flaming liability!'

From one viewpoint the watch could come down to just one more vendetta-style action against Adam Jennings. But the converse also mattered. How big a fool would openly drive past a hidden police check point he had personally set in operation?

'Am I suspended, sir?' Sergeant Imrie asked it glumly.

'You should be,' muttered Moss. 'From a rope, by the heels.'

Thane sighed, shook his head, and leaned back. If Imrie was suspended then the constable who'd been his partner in the car would have to go too. And if anything else turned up and more of the Braedale force were involved – well, the village would simply run out of police.

'You'll carry on. But one more piece of "helpfulness" to anyone and you'll wish you'd never been born.' He paused to let the warning sink home. 'How many people know about the checks on the farm?'

'Just the men on the station, sir. We've kept it quiet. We – well, we agreed that we'd better.'

That, at least, was good news. 'Who were at the meeting that night?'

'Well, all the cars were local. There were six of them – I've got the licence numbers and we know them anyway.' Imrie scratched his chin. 'I can be pretty certain about who was in them.'

'Make me a list.' Thane lit a cigarette and inhaled the smoke gratefully. 'Any idea if Fenn's daughter went there?'

'Not this time.' Imrie shook his head. 'There were only men in the cars. That's positive.'

Thane let him go, and the sergeant needed no encouragement. As the door closed, Moss gave a throaty laugh.

'What the hell's so amusing?' demanded Thane, scowling.

'Nothing – just my natural good humour breaking through,' soothed Moss. 'How'd you make out with Fenn?'

'Better than I expected – or maybe worse. I'm not sure which.'

Thane told what had happened at the bungalow and as he finished Moss nodded with a degree of sympathy. Then, after feeding a bismuth tablet into his mouth and sucking quietly for a moment, Moss asked, 'So what do we do now?'

'Stick to programme. See Jennings.'

Then, Thane promised himself, he was going to find somewhere quiet and try to get down to some straight thinking.

Away from any kind of bull, four-legged or otherwise.

*   *   *

The police Mini reached Broomvale Farm shortly after noon. Moss clinging to the rear seat, Thane up front with Constable Copeland as before, they drove north from the village for three miles then turned off down a length of rutted farm road heavily fringed with winter-gaunt leafless trees. The little white car bumped and swayed along, mud spattering against its sides, and emerged in a wide expanse of open grassland with the farm buildings ahead.

'Jennings lives in that?' Phil Moss shuddered at the notion. The main bulk of the farmhouse was a tall, bleak fortress of ancient, weathered grey stone. A small, modern extension had been added to one side in matching stone-work and there were equally modern barns and sheds visible behind it. But the overall effect was still forbidding. 'Hell, the place could qualify as an Ancient Monument!'

'It's sixteenth century, sir.' Constable Copeland broke an unusually long silence. The word had gone round the Braedale men that their visitors weren't in the happiest of moods. 'Mr Jennings bought it when he came up here about seven years ago. It was a ruin then – he spent a fair bit o' money doing it up.'

'I'd have knocked it down,' declared Moss fervently.

Thane chuckled softly, feeling the same way. Most of the windows in the main buildings were mere arrow-slits. The entrance was a narrow, gated archway. As a relic of the castle era all it lacked were a few Englishmen hanging in chains above that gate.

Or maybe Jennings preferred to keep such items at the back. Still smiling faintly, he pointed to a black Mercedes parked near the archway.

'His?'

'No sir.' Copeland was positive. 'He must have visitors.'

'And now he's getting more.' Thane waited until the Mini had stopped behind the other car. 'Copeland, how'd you like to earn your keep this time?'

'Sir?' Copeland switched off the engine and looked pleased.

'While we're seeing Jennings, take a walk around the back and have a gossip with the farmhands – anyone you meet. Try to find out if they've had any domestic trouble recently, and whether anyone has been fired or has quit his job. Understood?'

Constable Copeland nodded, and hoped he did.

The archway's wrought iron gate swung back on well-oiled hinges. Beyond it, the two detectives found themselves in a small cobbled courtyard with an atmosphere very different from Broomvale's grim exterior. Brightly painted flower boxes flanked a pair of old brass cannon. New, large windows had been cut in the freshly pointed stonework. Wiring cables ran discreetly to a scatter of overhead lights.

'Better,' muttered Moss. 'But I'll bet the drains still stink in summer.'

A modern bell-push was set to one side of a heavy, ornately carved oak door. They rang and waited. A middle-aged woman in a blue housekeeper's overall answered the summons, invited them in, and had them wait in a long, stone-floored hall. Then she vanished down a corridor.

'Nothing wrong with the heating,' murmured Thane, loosening his coat in the welcome warmth. He looked around. Rugs were scattered here and there on the polished floor, and the wood-panelled walls displayed a collection of old Scottish broadswords, targes and pipe banners. An antique oak chest, used as a telephone table, had all the appearance of being worth a year's pay.

'Think of the fuel bill for a place this size.' Moss hastily lowered his voice as the words echoed from the high ceiling. 'I've seen smaller museums.'

The housekeeper returned and they followed her along the corridor. She stopped at an opened door, tapped lightly, then ushered them on.

'Good to see you again – both of you.' Adam Jennings

crossed the room to meet them with a beam of welcome. He wore a blue sports shirt with brown slacks, his feet were in light tan moccasins, and he moved with an easy, supple energy. Thane tried to guess his age. With that mane of black hair he looked in his mid-thirties but was probably older.

They made polite noises, noticing a stranger in a blue business suit hovering in the background. Jennings had them peel off their overcoats and leave them on a chair.

'Nicely timed,' he declared in a brisk, satisfied rumble. 'Thane, I've someone here you'll want to meet.'

The stranger came forward on cue. He was small, ludicrously small beside Jennings' massive form. His face was round, with sharp eyes which glinted behind thick spectacles.

'Eric Lawson from International Fidelity Insurance,' introduced Jennings. 'And right now that's a company which owes me a sizeable packet of money.'

'Which we'll pay,' murmured Lawson. 'There's no dispute about it.' Then, for Thane's benefit, 'I'm here as claims superintendent for our north-east area.'

They finished the formalities and Jennings waved them towards the nearest chairs. His own choice was a deep leather job. Behind it on the wall, either by accident or design, was a full-sized portrait in oils. It showed him in a khaki shirt and dark tartan kilt against a symbolic background of rocks and heather.

Lawson produced a silver cigarette case and offered it around. Thane took one, accepted a light, and remarked, 'The insurance business must be prospering. That's a fairly smart car outside.'

'The Mercedes? Company issue – the prestige approach.' Lawson shook his head unhappily. 'After this little lot I'll be lucky if I rate a bicycle.'

Jennings gave a throaty, sympathetic chuckle and glanced at Thane. 'Making any progress on it, Chief Inspector?'

'A little – it takes time.' Thane had been looking around the room, which was furnished as a combination of study and office. An electric typewriter sat on a desk in the far corner and a TV set was recessed into the opposite wall with a cocktail cabinet near at hand. Another wall was lined with well-filled bookshelves.

If this dark-haired lazy-moving giant was the fanatic people claimed, he believed in being a comfortable fanatic.

'What about Fenn?' The name came harshly from Jennings' lips. For a moment the smile was wiped away.

'He's still at home, still suspended.' Thane shrugged in vague explanation. 'There's no charge against him – not so far.'

'You need proof before you go around charging people,' said Moss dryly. Half-hidden in the depths of a softly sprung couch, he leaned forward. 'Any kind of people, even police inspectors.'

Jennings nodded grimly. But International Fidelity's reaction was very different.

'Proof?' Lawson seized on the word like a pudgy terrier. 'Damn it, do you have to wait for a signed confession or something? From what I've heard you've got almost everything else!'

'They're being careful, very careful,' said Jennings with a trace of cynical amusement. His cool grey eyes considered Thane steadily. 'I don't blame you for it. But I thought that as Lawson was here it could give you a chance to check direct on the insurance aspect.'

'Fine.' Thane drew on his cigarette and used the nearest ashtray. 'What's the official position, Mr Lawson?'

'There's a claim and we'll meet it.' Lawson chewed his lips sadly. 'If you mean the background, we insure most of the herds in this area. Breeder protection policies are an International Fidelity speciality – one master policy covering a herd, premium rating depending on the quality of herd and the number of stock. The Marquis of Braedale came under the Broomvale Herd policy as just another bull until this American sale occurred.

'That made him something very special. We had to insist on switching him on to an individual policy.'

'Suppose the bull had died under the standard policy,' suggested Moss. 'Then what?'

Lawson shrugged. 'Then we'd have offered settlement at herd-standard valuation.' He glanced at Jennings. 'The Broomvale Herd are top quality. But that would still only have meant somewhere under £1,000.'

'And under the individual policy?'

'Very different.' The claims superintendent took off his spectacles and began polishing them earnestly on a hand-kerchief. 'The animal was bought for $120,000 subject to a contract of delivery to some obscure place in Texas. Cash on delivery – fit, live delivery, seller's risk till then. Special risk as far as my company was concerned. We agreed to offer death and accident cover, but only to approximately two-thirds live value – £35,000.'

'So I lose – well, call it either $40,000 or £15,000.' Adam Jennings reached inside his shirt with one hand and scratched the dark mat of hair beneath. 'Call it pounds. It sounds less that way.'

Lawson gave a suitably sympathetic nod. 'Well, I've advised you what we're doing. The moment Fenn is charged our lawyers move in.'

'Civil action for damages.' Jennings scratched on, his face impassive but the grey eyes suddenly icy. 'I've a lawyer all right. Whatever happens, Fenn will find that out.'

'Good.' Lawson cleared his throat. 'Anything more, Chief Inspector?' As Thane shook his head the claims superintendent got to his feet. 'Well, I'm finished here. I've seen the body, I've checked the ear-markings, taken a nose-print . . .'

'Eh?' Moss blinked and sat up.

'Nose-print – as in fingerprints.' Lawson gave a small,

secretive smile. 'Sometimes breeders aren't completely – ah – honest. They try to work a switch of animal. So we keep one nose-print on file in special cases like this, ready for comparison. But I'm not worried here. Our cheque's as good as in the post.'

He reached for his coat, a short, fur-lined gaberdine. As Adam Jennings helped him into it, towering over him in the process, Lawson had another thought.

'Oh, the carcase – you can get rid of it anytime as far as we're concerned.'

'Thane?' Looking over at him, Jennings raised a questioning eyebrow.

An inner caution made Colin Thane hesitate. Then he shook his head. 'Not yet. But soon – I'll let you know.'

Lawson buttoned his coat and glanced at his watch. 'Home in Edinburgh before dusk – yes, I'll make it. And if I can help, Chief Inspector, just telephone.'

He nodded and left, Jennings going along to see him out.

Phil Moss waited a moment then cautiously levered himself out of the couch and prowled the room. He stopped at the portrait, grunted under his breath, then moved over to the desk. Suddenly, he gave a low, soft whistle.

'Another of them, Colin. Looks like the de luxe version.'

Thane looked round. Silently, Moss lifted the small knife from the desk-top. It was the same in size to the ones they'd seen the previous night – the black bone handle, the short length of double-edged steel. But this one had a needle point, the butt of the handle was ornamented by a single blood-red stone held in a silver claw setting.

'It's a garnet stone, Inspector. Good-looking but nothing more.' Adam Jennings' deep voice chuckled unexpectedly from the doorway then he padded over, unperturbed. 'Like it?'

57

'It looks well enough made,' said Moss non-committally.

'It is,' said Jennings softly. 'And you hold no ordinary knife there.' He smiled a little as Moss quickly laid it down again. 'In the old Gaelic language they call it the *skean dhu* . . . the little black knife. I use it as the symbol and badge for my Children of the Mist.'

'Except theirs have rounded points,' murmured Thane. 'We've seen them.'

'That was your Inspector Fenn again.' Jennings combed both hands over his thick head of hair. 'He keeps on with the crazy obsession that I'm running some kind of Highland-style Mafia. But do you want to know why I chose the *skean dhu*?'

'Go on,' invited Thane, knowing they were going to get it anyway.

Jennings took a deep, swelling breath. 'Because there couldn't be a better symbol, a better reminder. Those silly little child-sized knives represent oppression.' His voice became softer, yet charged with earnestness. 'Physical oppression once – economic and political now. You're both Scots. You know what happened at Culloden – how the clans died fighting for freedom.'

Thane nodded slightly. Culloden was history-book stuff. He'd often wondered how many of those hairy-shanked Highlanders had been following a cause and how many had had their eye on the main chance of loot and pillage if they'd managed to reach London. Probably about fifty-fifty, if their descendants were any criterion.

'Freedom, Thane –' Jennings pronounced it like a bene-diction – 'but afterwards? Crushing oppression. If a Scot dared carry a weapon of any kind he was hanged. No more the broadswords, the Lochaber axe, the proud dirk. Yet even the English had to admit a man needed some-thing to cut his food, to use as a tool. So they sneered and said he could have a little knife. One so small it could live in a stocking. This –' his hand slapped down on the steel – 'this puny badge of servitude.'

'It was a long time ago,' said Phil Moss from the sidelines. 'The only equalizers that count now come in megaton grades.'

'I'm talking of people,' said Jennings impatiently. 'In terms of people we're still denied our rights as individuals and as a nation. Nobody's going to gift us what we want.'

'And what would you do?' asked Thane dryly. 'Take it, grab it?'

Jennings shrugged and gave a slow, cautious smile. 'Let's say work for it. I've learned to watch what I say. But I'll tell you this. The young are the people who understand best what I mean. They're not content to ask. They're not content to have a future programmed by some English computer.' He stopped and gave a short laugh. 'You're not here for any brand of political lecture. If you've questions about the Marquis better ask them before I start off again.'

'We've a few,' nodded Thane. 'Let's start with the Monday night. How many people were at this committee meeting?'

'Nine or ten – I can give you a list.' Jennings flipped open his desk pad and began writing. Without raising his head, he commented, 'They didn't hear or see anything. I've checked.'

'Did you?'

'No. Not till the next morning when Tommy Dougan, my head cattleman, came charging in with the news.' He finished the list, tore it from the pad, and handed it over. 'That's also when I heard that Dougan had seen Inspector Fenn out here. Dougan hadn't bothered about it at the time. He knew there was a meeting in the house. He thought . . .'

'I'll let him tell that part,' said Thane crisply. He folded

59

the list and put it away. 'Fenn's daughter, now – should she have been at the meeting?'

Jennings blinked and shook his head. 'No. She's a willing enough youngster. But this was committee business only.'

'Fenn apart, is there anyone else who'd have a big enough grudge against you?'

'Everyone makes the occasional enemy,' murmured Jennings. 'I quarrel with a few people. But no – this was a sick mind, Thane. And I'd say Fenn is sick that way.'

'If he is, we'll find out.' Thane got to his feet. 'Can we see where it happened – and meet Dougan?'

Jennings led the way, out of the room and down another long length of stone-flagged corridor.

'It's a bit of a rabbit-warren back here,' he apologized as they passed another arrow-slit window. 'But it was a lot worse when I came – half-ruined, most of the roof about to cave in. I had to get rid of the wet rot, clean out dungeons for the central heating plant then add a few luxuries like sanitation and electricity.'

They went through a door and emerged in the open at the rear of the building. Thane's nostrils twitched at the strong, warm farmyard smell and he heard Moss give a mutter of surprise.

Two long, low rows of roofed-in cattle pens lined a concrete walkway. They held a collection of young Angus cattle, stolid, thick-bodied black shapes of varying ages. Most were quietly feeding but an occasional snort sounded and some moved restlessly as the men walked past them.

Spotting an elderly farmhand carrying a bucket Jennings called him over and spoke briefly. The man nodded. As he went off, Jennings turned back to his visitors.

'I've sent for Dougan. I'll show you the place where it happened.'

He led the way again, past the pens and round the corner of the sprawling farmhouse block. In front of them, set on its own, was a small unit about the size of a tennis court. Fenced off, it had a brick shelter court at one end and a drinking trough at the other. Jennings opened a gate and they walked across more concrete to the shelter. The floor within had been swept, a mound of straw lay against the rear wall.

'Just here,' said Jennings, stopping. 'The Marquis was lying where I'm standing now. You've seen Sergeant Imrie's photographs?'

Thane glanced hopefully at Moss, who nodded.

Jennings scraped a pensive shoe along the floor. 'This is our isolation block. I had it built for animals waiting export clearance. The Marquis had been here nearly a month – only Dougan, myself and John MacGhee came inside.'

'But plenty of people would know the animal was here?' queried Moss.

Jennings nodded, putting a cigarette between his lips. 'And came to see him. He was a local showpiece.' He saw Moss looking around and added, 'Imrie searched for cartridge cases, anything else that might be evidence. He got nothing.'

Thane had been listening with only half his attention, thinking. 'We're close enough to the house. You're sure nobody heard the shot – or anything unusual?'

'Not a chance.' Jennings lit the cigarette, tossed the used match aside, and waved towards the one-time castle. 'Those walls run eight feet thick on this side – even more in places. And there was wind and rain on Monday night. If it had happened over at the main pens we might have heard and it is pretty certain the other beasts would have panicked. But not from here, not unless he used a grenade.'

They left the isolation block and walked back. A man was waiting at the main pens, leaning against one of the gates. He had short, fair hair and a thin face which hadn't seen a razor for a couple of days. He wore a long, stained leather waistcoat over a wool shirt and the legs of his moleskin trousers were tucked into the tops of heavy leather boots. Behind him, a young bull with a patch of white hair round one eye was making determined efforts to nuzzle his shoulder.

'Tommy . . .' Jennings beckoned.

The man brought one hand up in a half-salute but stayed where he was till they reached him.

'Police again,' said Jennings briefly, then turned to Thane. 'This is the man you want – Tommy Dougan, my head cattleman.'

Dougan managed something halfway to a smile. One of his front teeth was broken. He had a scar above his left eye, a thin white line of the kind which usually meant one Saturday night brawl too many. When he spoke, it was in a slow, cynical drawl.

'Well, mister? Do you want to ask questions or do I save time an' just tell it?'

'We'll try it your way,' said Thane curtly, feeling a fast-growing dislike for the man.

'It's best.' Dougan tucked his thumbs casually into the broad leather belt round his waist. 'Let's see, then. I live on the farm – got a place in the loft above the garage thanks to the boss here. Monday night I'd been down in the village till late on, then had to walk back – came in across the fields, the shortest way. Then I started round the house to the garage, in no mood for anything but to get my head down.

'That's when I saw Inspector Fenn, mister – though he didn't seem to see me. He was sneakin' away, heading back towards the road.'

'How near to him were you?' demanded Thane.

'Fifteen, twenty yards.' Dougan spat deliberately on the ground. 'I know. It was dark, wet, an' windy. And before you ask, I'd a skinful o' beer. But it was Fenn or someone damned like him, an' coming from the isolation block.'

Moss frowned. 'From the block or from that direction?'

Dougan shrugged. 'It's your problem, friend.'

Moss bristled, but Thane stopped him short. 'If you saw him, Dougan, why didn't you do something about it? Were you too – tired?'

'You mean drunk, right?' Dougan's watery blue eyes showed a momentary amusement. 'No. But I knew the boss had one o' his Home Rule meetings going on. There were cars parked all over the place out front, an' I just kind of decided Fenn had been there too for some reason.'

'Then had gone wandering off on his own?'

Dougan sighed. 'Mister, it didn't seem any of my business. Not then. Not till I found the Marquis in the morning.'

'At 6.30 a.m.,' nodded Jennings.

'Or near enough.' Dougan scratched his chin. 'First thing I always did was give him a look in. He jus' didn't move. Then I tried my toe in his ribs, a sort of tap. An' then –' he shrugged – 'then I saw what was wrong an' ran like hell to get the boss.'

It didn't take them much further. Thane pursed his lips. 'Let's get a couple of things straight. Where were you in the village?'

'Wi' – well, a friend, eh?' The man winked. 'An' she'd kick up hell if I said more.'

'You didn't speak to this man you thought was Fenn – speak to him or call out?'

'No.' Dougan shook his head wearily. 'Look, I was tired, mister. I wouldn't have given an extra blink if it had been half a dozen naked dancin' girls who were comin' that way.' He smirked a little. 'At least, I don't think so. Anything more?'

Thane shook his head. The cattleman nodded truculently and walked away. As he vanished among the lower pens Jennings gave a rueful chuckle and crossed to the gate. The white-patch bull sniffed loudly, prepared to back away, then settled as Jennings reached out and rubbed its polled head. At the same time he began talking softly to the animal.

'Are they all like that?' asked Moss, watching.

'Cattlemen or bulls?' murmured Jennings. He changed his stroking to the animal's moist black velvet muzzle. 'I won't speak for Dougan, though he knows his job. But if you mean bulls you're probably like most city-style innocents – with a built-in idea that a bull wants to flatten anything on two legs.'

'Well, don't they?' Thane remembered his far-back honeymoon in Spain. He'd taken Mary to the bull-fights – once. She'd threatened instant divorce if he even suggested it again.

'Depends on breed and temperament.' Jennings left the animal. 'Angus bulls are fairly placid. Some of the young-sters are skittish and it's just incidental that when they nudge you there's a lot of weight behind it. A full-grown bull with females can be dangerous occasionally. And big or small you don't fool around with them. But the average Angus is peaceful enough – that's one of their good points.'

Thane nodded. It meant that almost anyone could have walked across that pen with a gun in hand.

'Now –' Jennings glanced at his watch and made an apologetic grimace – 'if I can help more just say. But I've some people arriving soon. They're travelling up from Glasgow for a conference – Children of the Mist business. I'd like to be ready for them.'

'We won't stop you,' Thane assured him. As they set off round the house, Moss trailing a step or two behind, he asked, 'This conference – something special happening?'

Jennings nodded easily. 'We've final details to settle for a rally I'm holding there on Sunday evening. We've booked a hall and all the West of Scotland branches will be along – five, maybe six hundred members. If you'd like tickets . . .'

Hastily, Thane shook his head. 'Sorry. Even if we're finished here we'll have plenty to do.'

'Pity.' Jennings stopped as they neared the police Mini.

Constable Copeland was waiting with what was meant to be a patient expression.

'Well, if you change your minds let me know. Even policemen should be political animals. And believe me, what I've to say at Sunday's rally is going to be remembered – for a long time, Chief Inspector.' He smiled strangely and said it again. 'For a long time. Believe me.'

Chapter Four

Patience was a necessity Colin Thane had learned the hard way, learned without liking or really mastering it. As the police Mini gear-snatched away from Broomvale Farm he took one glance at their driver's young, earnestly controlled face and recognized the signs. Constable Copeland was trying hard to wait till he was asked, but he'd something on his mind.

Amused, Thane sat back and said nothing until the little car had travelled far enough to be out of sight of the farmhouse castle. Then he leaned forward and very deliberately switched off the ignition.

The engine died and the car coasted to a halt beside a tree. As they stopped, Phil Moss frowned and leaned forward.

'Anything wrong?'

'Not with me,' said Thane dryly. He turned to Copeland. 'All right, out with it. What happened?'

Copeland grinned with a self-conscious relief. 'I talked around like you asked, sir. Jennings has got rid of someone from the farm – and it was less than a month ago.'

Interested, Moss pulled himself still nearer.

'Who?'

'One of the cattlemen.' Copeland rubbed his broken nose with a pleased satisfaction. 'The story I got was that he'd a real ding-dong of an argument with Adam Jennings and was fired on the spot. He hasn't been seen since. The other farmhands think he left the area.'

'Do they?' Thane whistled tunelessly through his teeth for a moment, watching a rabbit which had popped out on the roadway just ahead. It stared back at him, too surprised to be afraid. Without moving his head, he asked the one-word question.

'Name?'

'Sam Hodge, sir. An old fellow and a pretty good worker. Nobody seems very sure what the row was about.' Copeland took a deep breath and ventured on. 'Hodge did most of the actual work involved in looking after the Marquis, according to the people I talked to back there. And if he went off with a grudge against Jennings . . .' He left the rest unsaid, waiting.

Thane chewed his lip, thinking, still watching the rabbit. Suddenly it stiffened, the long ears twitched, then it fled from some unseen danger. A moment passed before a slim, russet-coated weasel flickered across the road and vanished in pursuit.

'Did Hodge live on the farm?'

Copeland shook his head. 'No, he'd a room with a family called MacPherson. They've a cottage about midway between here and the village.'

Almost grudgingly, Moss cleared his throat. 'There's always the chance, I suppose . . .'

'All right,' said Thane quietly. 'You're the driver, Copeland. Let's find out.'

Copeland set the car moving.

It was a small stone cottage with white walls and windows which looked out across the fields towards the mountains. A few hens were scratching around a poultry run and a line of washing hung from a rope at the rear. They left Copeland in the car, walked over to the cottage door, and knocked. A woman's voice shouted a muffled reply from inside but the door remained closed.

Moss swore under his breath, shivered in the breeze, and used his fist again. This time it brought results. They heard hurrying footsteps then the door swung open and an irate face looked out.

'Now look, Peter, I've no time for . . .' The voice died away. Its owner, a woman with dark hair screwed up in pink plastic roller curlers, her hands white with flour, blinked and flushed.

'Mrs MacPherson?' Thane grinned at her confusion.

'Yes.' She flushed, and a hand went up in a vague attempt to hide the curlers. 'Och, I'm sorry. I thought it was that daft man of mine playing one of his tricks. He's due home about now.'

'Police, Mrs MacPherson.' Thane showed his warrant card briefly. 'We're trying to locate Sam Hodge.'

'You and me too.' The woman stiffened at the name. 'When he left here he owed me close on a month's rent. You'd better come in.'

They followed her through to a small, warm kitchen filled with the smell of fresh baking. Wiping the last of the flour from her hands, the woman considered them with a new interest.

'What's old Sam been up to that you're looking for him?' she demanded.

'Nothing we know about, but he might be able to help us,' said Thane warily.

'Aye.' She gave them a look of complete disbelief, noticed Moss eyeing a tray of home-baked scones, and pushed an empty plate towards him. 'Help yourself. You look like you need some fattening.'

Moss blinked but went ahead.

'Sam Hodge,' said Thane patiently. 'How long had he lived here?'

She thought for a moment. 'Near enough to three years, I suppose.'

'And when he left, did he say where he was going?'

The woman sniffed. 'He didn't say anything. The crafty old devil went out of here that morning cheery as you like.

I went into Braedale for some shopping in the afternoon, an' when I got back he'd packed and gone.'

'You mean –' Moss took another quick chew and swallowed a mouthful of scone – 'you mean you didn't see him again?'

'That's what I just said, isn't it?' Her mouth tightened indignantly. 'Three years here and then he does a thing like that to us. No rent, no note where he'd gone, not so much as an old sock left behind.'

'Did he have his own key?' asked Thane.

Mrs MacPherson was puzzled for a moment then understood. 'To get in, you mean?' A wisp of a smile crossed her face. 'Where are you from, Chief Inspector?'

'Glasgow C.I.D. – we're assisting the County force on a local case.'

'Aye.' Once again the word held its own inflections. 'Well, up here we don't bother much about locks or keys – except when the city folk are up during the summer. My door isn't locked. It wouldn't be neighbourly.'

Thane glanced wryly at his companion. Moss grinned and helped himself to another scone from the tray.

'Did he ever talk about relatives, write to anyone?'

She frowned. 'Well, there's a sister called Ethel down in Glasgow somewhere. She's not married and works in an office, I know that much. He always got a Christmas card from her but I've no address. Would you like to see his room?'

Thane nodded. She beckoned them out into the tiny lobby and pointed.

'Up those stairs, the door on the right. On you go – I've this oven to watch.'

They went up.

Sam Hodge's attic bedroom was small with a tiny window and a low ceiling. It had a bed and a chest of drawers and a few coatpegs had been screwed along one wall. The drawers were empty and the coatpegs bare.

'Like she said, it wouldn't be neighbourly to lock things

up.' Moss chuckled under his breath, still chewing. 'Well, he certainly didn't leave anything behind.'

Thane shrugged, crossed to the bed, and lifted the thin, lumpy mattress. His eyes met only bare, rusting springs.

'Cleaned out,' said Moss laconically. He turned to the window, glanced out, then drew back quickly with a low mutter of surprise. 'Ever get a feeling you're being watched? Take a look, Colin. But don't stick your big head too far out.'

Joining him, Thane squinted out and swore softly. The window was at a gable end of the cottage and gave a view of the road towards the village. The road curved in a series of gradual, climbing bends lined with thick hedge and from the attic's height they could see a familiar Land-Rover with a radio aerial. It had stopped about four hundred yards away, drawn in tight against the hedge. He could just make out a burly figure behind the wheel.

'MacGhee,' grunted Moss. 'Playing at cowboys and Indians. He'll be able to see Copeland and the Mini from there.' He gave an acid sniff. 'Looks like he's hoping to gather some gossip for his farmer pals.'

'Or Jennings.' Thane drew back frowning. 'Well, let's give them all something to talk about. I'd like a chance to take some of the local heat off Inspector Fenn and his family – till we're sure one way or the other, at any rate. Come on.'

They went back down to the kitchen and found Mrs MacPherson busy with more flour and a mixing bowl. She stopped as they entered, a hopeful expression on her face.

'If you find old Hodge will you let me know? That way I can get after him for the rent he owes.'

'You'll probably hear,' agreed Thane mildly. 'Do you have a photograph of him anywhere?'

She shook her head. 'No, but if it helps he's a wee fellow with grey hair and a moustache. And he's got a limp –

something to do with a war wound. He was in the Army for a spell, out in North Africa or somewhere.'

'Who cleaned his room?'

'I did.' She rested her hands on the edge of the bowl, her eyes hardening. 'But I don't pry into folks' private things, if that's what you're asking.'

'People wouldn't, not up here,' said Thane straightfaced. 'Still, you had to tidy around the room. Did you ever come across a gun among his things, Mrs MacPherson?'

'A gun?' Her mouth fell open.

'A gun,' he repeated. 'A small revolver, anything like that.'

She shook her head firmly. 'If he'd anything like that I'd have known. Unless . . .' She stopped and flushed a little.

'Unless what?' queried Moss, back at the tray of scones again.

'Well, he'd a sort of trunk he kept locked. He – everyone's got some private things, I suppose.'

'Even in Braedale,' murmured Thane. He signalled Moss, and his second-in-command came over with some reluctance. 'Thanks for helping us, Mrs MacPherson. If we do find him I'll let you know.'

She nodded and went back to the baking bowl.

Outside, they walked in casual fashion towards the Mini. But on the way Thane glanced quickly but carefully along the road. From ground level there was no sign of the Land-Rover waiting ahead.

'You baited that one nicely,' said Moss from the corner of his mouth. 'What's the betting MacGhee calls in to see her?'

'We'll find out.' Thane reached the Mini, opened the door, and gestured Moss into the rear. Then he climbed in and nodded to Copeland. 'Let's go. But don't rush it and be ready to stop when I tell you.'

The car purred off, heading along the winding road.

71

They were on the second bend beyond the cottage when the Land-Rover suddenly appeared coming towards them. John MacGhee gave them a cheerful wave as he passed.

Watching the rear window, Thane waited till the vehicle was out of sight. Then he had Copeland stop, got out quickly, and found a gap in the hedge where he could see the cottage.

The Land-Rover had stopped. John MacGhee climbed out, went over to the cottage door, knocked, and went straight in.

Thane smiled and headed back for the Mini. Once he was aboard, it started off again for the village.

They left Copeland at the police station, walked down to the Clachan Arms, and ate a late lunch. The food was half-cold, the service little better, but Colin Thane was too hungry to care.

Phil Moss felt differently. He toyed with an almost full plate of roast beef and soggy vegetables, remembering the dead bull lying a stone's throw away, beginning to regret the scones at the cottage. A familiar slow ache was beginning to gather low down under his ribs and he felt suddenly homesick for the noise and grime of Millside Division.

'Something wrong?' queried Thane.

He shrugged. 'Nothing special. I was just wondering what we were going to do about Hodge.'

Thane shook his head. He was wondering what they should do about a lot of things. And the Sam Hodge situation held a worry of its own. Did a man really sever roots three years old so quickly, so finally?

And even if Hodge meant another possible suspect in the ring it still left plenty of evidence against Fenn. Plenty for suspicion, for everything short of charging him.

'Colin –' Moss stopped, winced, and gave a long, low-keyed belch – 'how about this crazy idea that Jennings organized the raid on the War Department depot?'

72

'If Jennings wanted to blow something up that's the County's worry, not ours,' said Thane sardonically. 'At least we know he didn't shoot his own ruddy bull. He lost too much money in the deal – you heard what that insurance character said.' He shoved back his chair, suddenly impatient. 'Come on. It's time for another lesson on how to win friends and influence people. I'm going to put Sergeant Imrie and his happy band to work.'

Phil Moss sighed and rose, managing to slip another bismuth tablet into his mouth in the process. He patted his pockets to make sure he had more, then followed Thane out.

Still leading the way, Thane cut across the fringe of the village green and set a course towards the filling station. An elderly man in overalls was on duty at the pumps and greeted them with a quizzical nod.

'I'm looking for Dave Anderson,' said Thane shortly. 'Is he around?'

The man shook his head. 'Not right now. He took the afternoon off. Said he wanted to meet some people coming up from Glasgow.'

'At Jennings' place?'

'Uh-huh.' The man looked past him as a car drew in. 'Least, I suppose so. I know it's something to do wi' his Home Rule business. You'll get him later, though. He's usually playin' around in his wee workshop in behind here.'

'We'll be back,' promised Thane. He set off again, leaving Moss struggling to keep up with his long-legged stride.

'Hey –' he managed to draw level and stay there – 'what was that about?'

'Dave Anderson is the nearest thing we've met to a friendly Children of the Mist member,' reminded Thane. He grimaced. 'I'm going to find out just how friendly, Phil. Because if we don't get the kind of help we need I know

73

what's ahead. We're going to have to grill the Fenn family one by one – and that's a job I don't want.'

They reached the police station, went in, and nodded to the constable at the small inquiry desk. He mumbled a greeting then, as they passed, went scuttling off down a corridor.

It was easy enough to guess why. By the time they'd hung up their coats in what was usually Inspector Fenn's office they had Sergeant Imrie as a visitor.

'I heard you've been busy, sir.' Imrie forced a friendly smile in Thane's direction. 'Making much progress?'

Thane shrugged, sank into Inspector Fenn's chair, and lit a cigarette. 'Sergeant, let's put it this way. I've met people, I've talked to people, and right now I wish I'd never heard of Braedale. As far as I'm concerned you can take the whole damned district and dump it in the nearest ocean.'

'Yes, sir.' Imrie refused to be hurt. 'But you found out about Sam Hodge.'

'Copeland did,' corrected Thane. He pulled the desk pad nearer, found a pencil, and then looked up at the County man again. 'Anything through about Inspector Fenn's last official medical?'

Imrie nodded. 'I spoke to the Headquarters police surgeon. It was last May – all he found wrong with the inspector was a degree of nervous tension.'

Thane shrugged. If nervous tension was any guide to the potential criminal then half the male population should be locked up before nightfall. But it fitted with his own ideas about Charles Fenn. And seven, nearer eight months had passed since that examination.

He left the cigarette burning on an ashtray and scribbled busily for a few moments. Imrie watched him in silence, glanced inquiringly at Moss, and drew a warning head-shake.

'Right.' Thane let the pencil roll to one side, sat back, and gave a wintry grin. 'Sergeant Imrie, how well do you know the ladies of the village – the ones who're willing and able?'

Imrie raised an eyebrow but nodded. 'We've one or two. It depends on who asks them.'

'Tommy Dougan. He says he was with a woman till late on Monday night then walked home. I'd like to know who she was and when he left.'

'Bertha Sorren's his usual.' Imrie permitted himself a brief suspicion of a grin. 'We're a small enough place to know the local trade.'

'Check it.' Feeling in his pocket, Thane brought out a sheet of paper Adam Jennings had given him. 'Then put a couple of men on this. Jennings says it is a full list of the people who were at his committee meeting. I want formal statements from them all, no matter how little they know.' He paused, then snapped his fingers. 'While you're at it, make sure it matches with your own list for that night.'

'Easy enough, sir.' Imrie nodded and took the list.

'But this next one isn't.' Thane raised a warning forefinger. 'In fact, sergeant, that's why I'm giving it to you personally. I want Inspector Fenn's car and I want the clothes he was wearing that night. I want them brought back here. Then you'll have Copeland drive the car and the clothes down to Glasgow and take them to our Scientific Branch.'

Imrie licked his lips. 'Charlie Fenn won't like it.'

'I'm not so damned stupid as to imagine he would,' rasped Thane. 'Imrie, get this into your thick skull. Whoever shot the Marquis must have been damned nearly sitting on the brute's neck when he pulled the trigger. If there's animal hair, blood, anything else that matters on Fenn's clothes or that car he's in trouble. If there isn't – well, he's not in the clear. But it always proves something in his favour.'

Imrie ran a hand over his thinning hair and nodded glumly. 'I suppose so. What about the bullet and those photographs I took?'

'We'll keep them here.' Thane threw him a consolation. 'Tell your men to ask around for news of Sam Hodge – if he's been seen by anyone, heard from, anything at all.' Which, in turn, brought another thought. 'Just how many men do we have, anyway?'

'Including myself –' Imrie counted slowly on his fingers frowning – 'four here and two out wi' the patrol van who'll be back soon. And another two off duty till midnight.'

It was hardly an army, but it would have to do. Thane took a last draw on his cigarette, stubbed it, and glanced round.

'Anything missed, Phil?'

'Nothing we can't handle.' Moss had his back to them, studying an old Civil Defence poster on the wall. If civil defence was ever needed around Braedale somebody had their attack priorities wildly wrong. He read on, not bothering to look round. 'Sergeant, we've been here close on ten minutes. Where the hell's the tea?'

Imrie managed to grin a little and left promising it would be straight through. Once the man had gone Thane slumped back and swung his feet up on the desk.

'Sit down, Phil. You make the place look untidy.'

Wearily, Moss obeyed. His stomach was nagging like a high-grade toothache, he mentally cursed all home bakers and his own stupidity. Pressing one hand against his front he waited.

'Phil –' Thane looked at him again, changed his mind about asking how bad it was, and tapped the desk instead – 'we'll split the rest. I'll need to make some kind of report to Buddha Ilford for a start. Then I'm going to mop up a few bits and pieces.'

'Including Hodge?' queried Moss. 'There's his sister in Glasgow.'

Thane nodded. 'I'm landing that in Ilford's lap. But Fenn is still number one. I want to know more about his family, particularly the daughter – not from here but from further back.'

'A digging job.' Moss grunted his understanding. 'I'll start with County Headquarters and his Assistant Chief Constable pal. Mind if I check on this explosives business while I'm at it?'

'Suit yourself. But there's more waiting. I want . . .' He broke off at the sound of a light tap on the door. Constable Copeland came in carrying two half-pint mugs of tea and set them down carefully.

'Will you need me for a spell, sir?'

'Not as long as the car's available.' Thane sipped the tea. Like all police station brews it tasted like it had been boiled for a fortnight. 'Sergeant Imrie told you about the Glasgow trip?'

Copeland nodded. 'He's on his way to Inspector Fenn now. I've to get hold of Bertha Sorren.'

Moss belched, felt better immediately, and managed a chuckle. 'Remember your safety drill when you're there and keep the door open behind you – she might feel like a change of company.'

'But not with me, Inspector.' The young cop's face twisted in a rueful grin and he tapped his flattened nose. 'Bertha gave me this a couple of years ago when I booked her on a drunk and disorderly charge. She spun quite a story in court about how the bottle just slipped in her hand.'

He went out, still grinning, and closed the door behind him.

Taking another swallow from the mug Thane returned to his list. 'Fenn first, Phil. Then back to Sam Hodge – I want to know more about the quarrel he had with Jennings.' He rubbed his chin, uncertain on this one. 'Let's try to steer clear of asking Jennings direct. Who else could we try?'

'The vet,' suggested Moss. 'MacGhee was going out

there most days. He'd probably hear why Hodge wasn't around any more.'

'Ask MacGhee and he'll probably run straight to Jennings.' Thane thought for a moment. 'How about MacGhee's assistant?'

'Margaret Linton?' Moss sat upright and gave a surprisingly enthusiastic nod. 'That's a better idea. She might know, and I don't think she'd talk. If I got her on her own . . .'

'Then remember your advice to Copeland,' said Thane dryly. 'Keep the door open.'

Moss sniffed indignantly. 'She's a professional woman, Colin.'

'They're worse than the amateurs,' murmured Thane. 'And being used to sick animals, she might like the idea of taking on a frail, middle-aged liability – it's what they call the mothering instinct.'

Moss swore under his breath, rose bleakly from his chair, and scowled down.

'Any more helpful advice?' he queried.

'No, but I'm always available,' grinned Thane.

'Away to hell,' said Moss. He went out, muttering to himself about the parentage possibilities of divisional Chief Inspectors.

Left alone, Colin Thane lit a fresh cigarette and knew that he could now ignore Phil Moss's activities until that thin, baggy-suited individual decided to report back.

Give Moss a real job of burrowing to do and he set his own pace, happily in his element. Reports, statistics, toothcombing through documents or patiently tracking down the apparently trivial – sometimes Thane envied his second-in-command's gift of persistence.

He had no illusions about his own less patient approach. He knew the rules, he'd disciplined himself to follow them most of the time, he'd take scientific aid – or any other kind of aid – if it looked like helping.

But in the end Colin Thane's kind of police work still

78

often came down to backing a hunch, acting on it, then waiting and hoping.

Phil Moss was the balance. By not worrying about working under a younger man. By possessing a grey gift of insolence. By usually having at least one idea in reserve if Thane's original plans went wrong – an idea which constituted a second chance for the head of Millside Division.

And even if Moss preferred words to deeds, he could still shove the bookwork aside and use a baton on a Saturday night back street, his wiry frame equally at home in that bloodier element.

Headquarters made plenty of mistakes. But Colin Thane knew he'd plenty of reason to bless the day the decision had been made to team them together as a new, unlikely partnership for Millside – Thane straight from a spell with the regional crime squad, Moss wanting a change from being a Headquarters special duty man.

Still, Millside Division was a long distance away for the moment. Humming quietly to himself, Thane lifted the telephone. When the desk constable answered he asked for a line and told the man to leave it that way.

Then he began dialling.

Getting hold of Buddha Ilford was easy enough. Mid-afternoon was when the city C.I.D. chief usually got rid of his paperwork. Thane suffered through a minute or so's initial joviality about holidays in the country, gave Ilford a brief summary of what he'd done, then got down to what mattered.

'I need to locate this cattleman, Hodge, sir. If we could get a lead through his sister . . .'

'Ethel, single, works in an office in town.' Ilford's voice didn't hold too much hope. 'I've got that. We'll try. But you think Fenn's holding out. Meaning if he didn't do it he knows who did?'

Thane grimaced at the receiver, cursing Ilford's attempt at simplification. 'Maybe. We're working on it.'

'Another way of saying you don't know,' grunted Ilford dispassionately. 'Feel happy about Jennings?'

'On the insurance side, yes,' agreed Thane. 'That seems genuine.'

'It is,' said Ilford shortly, clearing his throat in a pontifical way which sounded like a thunderstorm in Thane's ear. 'I thought I'd find that out for myself, checked with International Fidelity's head office. They've been in touch with the American buyers. The transaction was positive till the bull was shot. Now it's dead as mutton – if you'll pardon an inept phrase.'

Thane managed what was meant to be a laugh. 'Jennings will be in Glasgow on Sunday. He's making a speech somewhere.'

'Special Branch know about it,' said Ilford with a touch of weariness. 'This Children of the Mist outfit have rented the city Concert Hall for the night. God knows what they're up to, but they're organizing press conferences and TV interview sessions for afterwards and promising they'll make headlines. Special Branch are in a mild panic wondering what's going to happen.'

'If I hear anything I'll pass it on,' promised Thane. 'How are things at Millside Division?'

'Call it an ominous quiet,' said Ilford shortly. 'Hertson's there. I've only spoken to him once today and he didn't sound too happy – started twittering about insubordination.'

Thane winced. It seemed as good a moment as any to ask for Criminal Records. Ilford transferred the call, hung up, and the Headquarters switchboard kept Thane waiting for what seemed an age before putting him through.

He knew the policewoman who answered. Her name was Marybelle, she was a sergeant, looked like an angel and had a judo black belt in her bottom drawer.

He explained what he needed. 'Routine search for a Samuel Hodge and a Thomas Dougan. Nothing known this end, Marybelle. Hodge is small, grey-haired, middle-aged. Dougan is fair-haired, blue eyes, medium-height, an old scar above the left eye.'

She asked him to hang on. He sighed and settled back, knowing it might take time. Away in the background distance he could hear a typewriter rattling and another phone bell ringing. Then, fast and loud, the clattering rhythm of a card-sorting machine.

If Hodge or Dougan had any kind of police history the machine should be able to find it. Glasgow's Headquarters building housed the central Scottish Criminal Records collection – which was a reasonable location, since the majority of neds and assorted villains on file had been born within a five-mile radius of the place.

S.C.R.O. was the ultimate destination of a constant torrent of forms, photographs, reports and case histories. One long bank of card-file cabinets indexed close on a quarter million criminal conviction records, the next-door offences conviction records adding another 130,000 names to the total.

Yet between them they were only a beginning. The Department sheltered Modus Operandi section, with another quarter million names carded. If you preferred pictures, Photo Index had 60,000 on tap . . . with others out on loan to Wanted Persons, while Missing Persons kept complaining about lack of space.

All that, and the Scientific Branch's fingerprint collection as an extra which ran to another 200,000 cards. Someday, the police committee promised, the whole lot was scheduled to be computer programmed.

When there was money.

If ever there was money.

Thane rocked wearily in his chair, and smoked his way through another cigarette while the card-sorter kept up its staccato bursts of activity.

At last the machine fell silent. There was a pause, then

81

he heard Sergeant Marybelle humming to herself as she picked up the receiver.

'Still there, Chief Inspector?'

'Yes.' He levered himself upright and held a pencil ready.

'Samuel Hodge, aged fifty-seven –' she chuckled a little – 'he looks rather a nice wee thing. One conviction only, ten years ago. Six months for breach of the peace, malicious damage, assault, attempted assault on the police and damaging a patrol van. It sounds like he had a one-man riot to himself.'

Which probably meant a night on red wine and heavy beer. Thane told her to advise Buddha Ilford then asked, 'What about Dougan?'

'That's not so easy.' She sounded slightly annoyed. Criminal Records usually did when they couldn't give a straight answer. They prized their image of infallibility. 'You couldn't give me more details?'

Thane sighed. 'Like what? His size of shirts?'

'Very funny, sir.' Her voice chilled several degrees. 'We happen to have eight Thomas Dougans on file. Allowing for age we're still left with three who have fair hair, blue eyes and some sort of scar.'

'Above the left eye?' He found it hard to believe.

'Two of them, yes.'

Thane swore under his breath. 'How soon can you produce photo-copy sets on all three?' He heard her turn and speak to someone else in the room, then she came back on the line.

'An hour or so, Chief Inspector.'

'All right,' he agreed. 'Organize them for me. There's no real rush, but I'll have a Perth County man collect them this evening.'

He hung up, shook his head at his luck, then decided he might as well get the next call over and done with. It took even longer – the British Army might be a highly

82

mechanized force, but their office staff still operated as if they were sorting out the aftermath of Waterloo.

Eventually, he succeeded. A brisk-voiced major in Scottish Command headquarters, Edinburgh, promised that Army Records would be put on the job of digging up the files on one former Black Watch sergeant Charles Fenn and one infantryman, Samuel Hodge, regiment, rank, serial number unknown but with possible North African service.

'Though not right away, old fellow,' drawled the Army voice. 'Too late in the afternoon, you know. Sometime tomorrow, eh?'

Thane glanced at his watch as he thanked him and ended the call. It was nearly 4 p.m., time to find out what the rest of his makeshift team were doing. Going out of the smoke-filled room, he wandered down the corridor until he came to a small, empty cell-block. He came back again, heard voices, looked round a half-opened door, and the talk died. It was the police station storeroom, racks of equipment lining the walls – and, judging by the slightly guilty faces turned in his direction, it was also a useful hideaway. Sergeant Imrie was there, tunic unbuttoned and a pipe stuck in his mouth. So was Copeland, sprawled on a bench with his hat over his eyes. Another cop he hadn't seen before had been filling a row of cups from a steaming kettle.

Copeland scrambled upright. The cop with the kettle stiffened. Only Imrie stayed as he was, sucking the pipe.

'Just looking around,' Thane told them mildly. He glanced at the cups. 'Any to spare?'

Imrie took the pipe from his mouth. 'One for Mr Thane, Alex,' he said briefly. 'Inspector Moss is still out.'

Thane raised an eyebrow.

'On inquiries, he said.' Imrie shrugged his ignorance of what that might mean. 'He borrowed the Mini and told me he might be an hour or so.'

The cop with the kettle brought over a filled cup. It was

83

coffee, the instant variety and heavily sugared. Thane settled on the bench.

'You've seen Inspector Fenn?'

Imrie nodded. 'His car is outside and the clothes are in the back. He said to tell you the tank's full and he wants it that way when it comes back.'

'I'll remember,' promised Thane, curbing a grin.

He went through the rest with them. Bertha Sorren had more or less willingly confirmed that Dougan had left her place soon after midnight. All but two of the names on the list Adam Jennings had given him had been contacted. None had seen or heard anything which could help. And there was no word anywhere of Sam Hodge's possible whereabouts.

Deliberately, he lingered and talked around the situation with the local men. They thawed gradually, were still cautious, but at least he had the feeling the antagonism had begun to melt. Copeland would pick up the Records package once he reached Glasgow, leave Fenn's car there, and take a train back to Perth. Sergeant Imrie promised to arrange for a County Headquarters car to collect him there and bring him out.

'Which will mean about midnight when he gets here,' warned Imrie. 'If you need another driver before then . . .'

'We shouldn't,' Thane told him. 'I'm not planning on travel till I've got a tidier picture from here.'

He left them, collected his coat, and went out. Inspector Fenn's car, a small red Ford, was parked beside a patrol van. Going past them, he walked through the gathering dusk towards the centre of the village then turned in the direction of the filling station.

A new face, a girl, was on duty at the pumps. She directed him round the back of the tin-roofed garage building and he knocked on the door of a small wooden hut which had bright light streaming from its windows.

Dave Anderson let him in. The lanky young redhead was in his shirt sleeves, and most of the hut's interior was

84

packed with a debris of old TV tubes and radio components. An electric soldering iron rested on a workbench beside the innards of a transistorized car radio.

'Call it a sideline – I can use the extra money,' explained Anderson cheerfully. He cleared a stool for Thane by the simple expedient of dumping a bundle of technical magazines on the floor. 'I heard you'd been looking for me.'

'This afternoon – there was no rush.' Thane looked around him, noting the surprisingly wide range of test equipment. 'Did it begin as a hobby?'

'This?' Anderson nodded. 'I got interested when I was doing my degree course at Strathclyde.' His mouth crinkled. 'Don't look so surprised, Chief Inspector. My folks said I had to have a university education. But they didn't say I had to use it – and I don't like cities.'

'That's your business.' Thane perched himself on the stool. 'Dave, you told me last night I could come round and talk.'

'About Sylvia Fenn?' Anderson found his cigarettes, gave one to Thane, put another in his mouth, then lit them both with the tip of the glowing soldering iron. 'Like I told you, she's a nice kid. Wild, but nice. When she lands in trouble . . .'

'Is she in trouble?' Thane let the smoke trickle slowly from his lips. 'You talked to her this morning.'

Anderson shrugged non-committally. 'I talk to her most mornings. She'd come down to collect some groceries.'

'That's not what I asked.'

'I know.' Anderson pursed his lips. 'Anything she told me was private, personal – and nothing to do with whether her old man shot the Marquis.'

Colin Thane considered the thin young face opposite. 'Charlie Fenn may not be popular with the Children of the Mist,' he said slowly. 'But he still deserves the benefit of truth. Did anything happen at that committee meeting, Dave – anything I should know about?'

A strange flicker crossed Anderson's face. Then he shook his head. 'Nothing. And Sylvia wasn't there.'

'All right.' Thane gauged the youngster's stubbornness and probed round it. 'You were at Adam Jennings' place this afternoon?'

Anderson nodded. 'Meeting some people – you know about them, according to Adam. We're taking a couple of bus-loads of Children from here to Glasgow for the rally. That's why I was along.'

'Did he mention Sam Hodge?'

'No.' A grin slid over Anderson's lips. 'But I know Sergeant Imrie has been asking around. Sam's a funny little character. But wherever he is now he wouldn't chop the Marquis – he damned nearly worshipped the beast.'

Thane had a depressing feeling he wasn't getting anywhere. But he tried again. 'I know how Charlie Fenn feels about Jennings. I'm not completely sure why. Could one reason be that he thinks Sylvia is – well, something special as far as Adam Jennings is concerned?'

Anderson blinked then laughed aloud. 'If Fenn thinks that he's even crazier than I imagined. Adam's no saint, but if he pats Sylvia on the head occasionally it's just to stir up more trouble for Fenn.'

'You think he should?'

'Chief Inspector, I think my own way about a few things.' Anderson combed his fingers through his unruly hair. 'The thing that matters is that Adam Jennings has a – well, a touch of magic about him. He's a leader, the kind the Home Rule movement needs to fan things along.'

'Fan things into a fire?' Thane chose his words carefully. 'Suppose he wanted to use force – all-out force. Blow up something, organize a riot somewhere. How would you feel then?'

Anderson looked down at the workbench for a moment. Then, slowly, he shook his head. 'There's more than one way of fighting for what you want, Chief Inspector. Maybe

86

Adam still has to find that out. But plenty of the rest of us know it. When . . .' He stopped and quickly corrected himself. 'If things start happening what we'll do will be very different from what anyone expects. No blood, no bombs – and no need for batons, believe me.'

'Let's hope you mean it, Dave.' Thane rose from the stool, knowing he wasn't going to make any further progress. 'Well, if you change your mind about anything . . .'

'It still wouldn't help you, my word on it.' Anderson opened the door for him. 'I'll ask around about Hodge for you, though. That's a promise.'

The door closed as Thane left. Night had arrived, cloudy, cold, with little moon. He walked slowly along the quiet village street, glancing in the few shop windows which were still lit, pondering exactly what to do next.

The sight of the white police Mini lying outside the Clachan Arms decided that for him. Thane went into the hotel, decided to try the bar first, and looked in.

Not long open, the place was almost empty. But a table in the far corner was occupied – he crossed over, hiding his surprise, and met Phil Moss's faintly embarrassed gaze. Sitting opposite Moss was Margaret Linton. She had a gin and tonic in front of her, Moss's glass held a dark, king-sized port.

'Hello, Colin.' Moss grinned weakly. 'I found our lady vet.'

'Who didn't really know she'd been lost.' Margaret Linton's eyes twinkled. The white overall had gone. She had a tan leather coat draped over her shoulders and wore a pastel green wool two-piece suit. The soft lighting of the bar made her look younger, banished the grey from her hair. 'Won't you join us, Mr Thane?'

He beckoned the barmaid, ordered a whisky, then brought the drink over and sat beside them.

'I – uh – went to John MacGhee's place,' said Moss uneasily. 'He was out, but Margaret was more or less

87

closing up for the night. She needed a lift back to the village – her car is in for servicing right now. So I thought – uh – we might as well come back here and talk.'

'In comfort?' Thane nodded blandly. 'Good idea. Better than your usual style.' He ignored Moss's glare and turned to Margaret Linton. 'I suppose he did get round to asking you about Sam Hodge?'

'Yes.' She sipped her drink. 'I knew Hodge had gone. John told me he turned up drunk for work once too often and Adam Jennings sent him packing.'

'No row?'

'There probably would be.' She glanced at Moss's hardly touched glass. 'Phil, you should take that, really. I told you – port's full of iron, but low on acid. There's nothing better for the system.'

'Old wives' tale?' queried Thane as Moss took an obedient gulp.

'Scientific fact,' she corrected firmly. 'The next best thing to a blood transfusion. I've even used it on pregnant cows and found it helped. If I dealt in people – well, with someone like Phil I'd throw every medicine overboard and concentrate on a balanced diet plus a few glasses of port a day.'

'I'm not pregnant,' spluttered Moss feebly.

'Maybe not, but you've an ulcer,' she reminded breezily. 'What's more, you're of mature years and living alone. You need a more organized regime.'

'True,' murmured Thane, deciding that Margaret Linton certainly didn't waste time when it came to gathering facts. Across the table, Moss took a deep breath and quickly changed the subject.

'Anything been happening, Colin?'

'Not much. I called Buddha Ilford and he made impatient noises.' Thane shrugged his acceptance. 'And you?'

'A couple of things,' said Moss cautiously with a glance at Margaret Linton. 'Nothing important but – well, interesting. They'll keep. I – uh – was wondering, though. If

we're not pushed we could maybe give Mar . . . Miss
Linton a meal here then I'd drive her home.'

Thane blinked and tried to hide his surprise. The last
time he could remember Phil Moss buying a woman a
meal it had been pie and beans at an all-night coffee stall
– just before he nailed her on a soliciting charge.

Margaret Linton frowned. 'Maybe I'd better not . . .'

'Go ahead,' he told them, straight-faced. 'But I'll have
to leave the honours to Phil. I've a couple of reports to
write.'

Moss gave him a look compounded from equal parts of
suspicion and gratitude. But he finished his drink, rose,
and left them before any argument could begin.

Sergeant Imrie was holding the fort on his own when
Thane got back to the police station. The patrol van had
gone out to deliver some Traffic Court summonses round
the local farms, the last two men on Adam Jennings' list
had been contacted with negative results, and the rest of
the world was unchanged.

Thane left him, went back to Fenn's office, and settled
down behind the desk.

Lighting a cigarette, he chuckled to himself again over
Phil's startling behaviour. Well, he'd given him a clear field
– but even if he didn't yet have a report to write it was
time he got some of the confusion down on paper.

He'd been working for about twenty minutes when the
telephone rang. He lifted the receiver warily.

'Thane.'

'And Mrs Thane.' Mary's voice came cheerfully over the
wire. 'How are things in the far north?'

'Sticky. So far, anyway.'

She made a sympathetic noise. 'And Phil?'

'I'd say he's enjoying himself.' He decided to keep just
why for later.

'Well, we're fine. But –' her manner changed – 'Colin,
you've probably got worries enough. Still, you'd better

89

know. It's Chief Inspector Hertson. He's making things difficult in the Division.'

'What's happened?' he asked easily. 'Mutiny or open warfare?'

'Be serious.' She wasn't amused. 'I've had a call from – well, from someone.' Which meant the Millside switchboard girls. 'Look, I know young Michael Beech rubs you the wrong way. But he's been suspended by Hertson. Something to do with Beech being insolent – which I don't believe.'

'Maybe not.' He sighed. 'Still, Beech has a natural gift for rubbing people the wrong way. And for surviving.'

'Meaning it doesn't matter?' Her voice held an angry protest.

'Hertson's running things till I get back,' he reminded gently, then relented. 'All right, pass the word that I'll square it with Buddha Ilford when I get home. And tell them I hope they'll remember what a mild, easy-going character they've usually got around.'

Mary said a word he didn't think she knew. 'When will you be back anyway?'

'Before the Monday concert,' he assured her.

When he said goodbye a little later he thought for a moment about calling the Division direct. But that wouldn't really help. Shrugging, he got down to work again.

The last page of notes was nearly finished when Thane heard a tap on the door. He glanced up as Sergeant Imrie entered.

'Sir –' the County man seemed oddly puzzled – 'I've got Mrs Fenn and her daughter outside. They want to see you but won't say why.'

Suddenly hopeful, Thane pursed his lips and nodded. By the time Imrie had returned with the women he'd deliberately moved away from Fenn's desk and greeted them just inside the door.

'Thank you for seeing us.' Isobel Fenn spoke quietly in

a tired voice. Her daughter hung back a little, saying nothing, her head low. Glancing past them, he gave a slight motion of his head. Sergeant Imrie went out, closing the door reluctantly.

'Sit down,' he invited.

'We'll stand, I think.' Isobel Fenn wore an old tweed coat, buttoned to the neck. Her hands clutched a small leather purse. 'It won't take long, Mr Thane. I've – we've come to tell you why my husband is behaving like an idiot.'

'I'm listening,' he said softly, waiting.

'And this time it's the truth.' She gripped her daughter by the arm and pushed her forward. 'That's right, isn't it, Sylvia?'

The girl nodded, quailing before her mother's chill determination.

'The start's easy enough,' said Isobel Fenn in the same tired, resolute voice. 'Sylvia told us she had to go to a special Children of the Mist meeting at Adam Jennings' farmhouse on Monday night. Her father said no – which meant the usual shouting and tears before he said yes. But she was to be home by eleven-thirty, or else.' She stopped for a moment, her mouth a tight, angry line. 'We sat up till twelve-thirty. Then Charlie went out. He said he was going to Broomvale and that if necessary he'd drag her out of the place.'

Thane nodded, saying nothing, guessing part of what was coming.

'She wasn't there. Charlie came back about one-thirty – he'd looked in a window, saw the meeting still going on, and she just wasn't there. When she did walk in it was almost 3 a.m.' She pushed her daughter forward again. 'Tell him where you were. Or you know what's waiting when we get home.'

Sylvia Fenn swallowed hard. 'I – I was out with some-one. In a car. We – we went down to Perth for a few drinks.'

91

'Someone?' Thane glanced from the girl to her mother.

'He's married,' said Isobel Fenn shortly. 'A stupid young idiot wi' a nice young wife and two children not school age. And his wife's worried enough without knowing this. He's in hospital and the car's a wreck.'

It clicked. 'Sergeant Imrie was on his way to a road accident that night. The same one?'

'Aye.' Isobel Fenn's voice was dry. 'But Imrie doesn't know it.'

'We were late leaving Perth,' said her daughter slowly, the words little more than a whisper. 'Then – well, we were going too fast. The car skidded and – and we hit a tree. I wasn't hurt, but he was, his legs and face. There was another car coming and he told me to run.'

'Why?' asked Thane quietly.

'He – we didn't want to be found together.'

'So she ran,' said her mother grimly. 'And I'm the one who got the story out of her, thanks to a good leather belt. Not Charlie – he makes a big noise but he wouldn't lift a hand to this one, not if she'd committed murder.' She gave a slow, helpless shrug. 'That's what happened, Chief Inspector.'

Tough, obstinate Charlie Fenn – struggling to keep his kid out of a mess, in an even bigger one himself. Thane spared a moment to thank the Lord he didn't yet have a teenage daughter.

'And the bull?'

'It wasn't Charlie,' said Isobel Fenn, her head coming up. 'The only gun he's ever owned is that .22 rifle. And the rifle's why I'm here, no matter what I promised. You took his car and his clothes –' she saw the explanation framing on his lips and stopped it with a quickly upraised hand – 'and we knew why. It was needed. But it hurt. So after a while Charlie said he was going to do the one thing that would prove he was right – prove it and still keep Sylvia's name out of things.'

Thane frowned. 'Prove he was right? How?'

She shook her head. 'All I know is he's been gone since dusk. And fifteen minutes ago I found the rifle had gone with him. That's – that's why I'm here.'

Because she was afraid, without being sure why. He saw it in her eyes, in the way those hands gripped the purse as if they'd never let go.

He lifted his coat from the wall-peg. 'Let's find out if he's back yet, Mrs Fenn.'

They went out of the police station past a bewildered Sergeant Imrie, the girl trailing a step or two behind. Isobel Fenn said nothing on the short walk to the bungalow. A light burned in her front window and as they drew near a uniformed figure came out of the shadows in the garden. As Thane frowned, then remembered the watch he'd ordered on the house, the constable came over and saluted.

'Any sign of Inspector Fenn coming home?'

The man shook his head. But Isobel Fenn moistened her lips, still hoping.

'He – there's always the back way.' She left them and went into the house.

Sylvia stood at Thane's side, silent and uneasy. A minute passed, then her mother appeared again in the doorway, shook her head, and went back in again leaving the door still open.

'She needs you right now, Sylvia,' said Thane quietly. The girl swallowed, nodded, and hurried up the path. As she went, he turned to the waiting constable. 'If he shows up, I want to know – straight away.'

Before the man could answer he was striding back towards the station.

Sergeant Imrie was speaking on the telephone at the inquiry desk as he went in. The County man saw him, gave a sharp grunt of relief, and held out the receiver.

'Inspector Moss, sir – for you. He says it's urgent.'

Thane took the receiver quickly. 'Phil?'

Moss's voice echoed tensely over the line. 'I'm out at MacGhee's place. Came out with Margaret Linton. You'd better get over, Colin. MacGhee's dead. Somebody shoved one of those *skean* knives through his throat.'

'I'll come,' said Thane mechanically, and hung up.

Chapter Five

John MacGhee lay like some macabre centrepiece on the wood-tiled floor of his surgery, a centrepiece surrounded by a confusion of overturned furniture, smashed equipment and scattered papers.

A trail of blood had spattered its way across his desk and the floor, smaller droplets mottled the walls. It was a trail which, inevitably, led to its source – the small, deep wound in the dead man's throat. Like a river in spate, blood had also soaked down the front of his shirt and jacket and spread beneath him in a congealing pool.

'It must have been a ding-dong of a fight,' mused Phil Moss with a clinical interest.

Colin Thane nodded bleakly and bent over the veterinary surgeon's body, taking in one detail at a time, mind functioning in a cold, precise isolation.

But the rest of him felt sick.

Violent death came any city Divisional chief's way with reasonable regularity. But Thane always loathed these first few moments, the initial shock and need for adjustment created by murder and what it left behind – particularly when the victim was anyone he'd known even slightly in life.

He'd driven out through the cold night darkness with Sergeant Imrie and two constables in the hastily recalled patrol van. When they'd arrived, the bungalow had been a blaze of light with Moss's borrowed Mini parked outside.

Pale-faced but outwardly calm, Margaret Linton had let them in.

To meet this.

John MacGhee lay as he had died, one leg twisted under him, the left hand frozen in a final, clawing movement towards his neck. The wound was low on the left side of the throat, little more than a narrow, crusted slit in the flesh.

But there were other, lesser injuries which told their own story. MacGhee's fat, death-sagged face had smashed lips and a shallow graze high on the left cheek. Part of the blue sports jacket's collar was ripped and torn. Thane considered MacGhee's hands, noted the small, ragged cut high on the palm of the right, then slowly got to his feet.

'The knife, Phil?'

Moss pointed. The *skean dhu* lay a few feet from the body, half-hidden by the overturned examination table. There was blood on the bright steel, from the needle-sharp tip up to the start of the black bone hilt. And, like the *skean dhu* they'd seen at Adam Jennings' home, it had an ornamental claw setting at the haft end – but this time the stone was a polished chip of white, blue-veined quartz.

'His, according to Margaret,' volunteered Moss. 'He used it as a letter-opener – usually kept it around his desk, like Jennings. Want my side of what happened?'

'In a minute.' Thane beckoned Sergeant Imrie over from the doorway. 'Where's Miss Linton now?'

'Waiting in her office, sir.' Sergeant Imrie made a stoical attempt to keep his manner everyday. 'I left one man with her and the other constable is with the patrol van. Eh . . . I'd a quick look around outside, sir. There's no sign of MacGhee's Land-Rover.'

'Phil?' He drew a headshake from Moss and swung back to Imrie. 'Has she a phone in her room?'

Imrie nodded.

'Ask her to come here. Then call County Headquarters. Tell them we'll need the usual back-up assistance – and

96

I want an immediate general alert circulated for Charlie Fenn and that Land-Rover. Get the vehicle registration number from Margaret Linton.'

Imrie swallowed hard but said nothing and turned to go. Suddenly, Thane swore and called him back. 'Before you contact Headquarters better phone Adam Jennings at Broomvale. Warn him he could have a visitor too and say we'll get a couple of men up there as soon as we can spare them. Meantime, put the two you've got to work – I want any outbuildings searched.'

'Yes sir.' Sergeant Imrie nodded grimly and left.

'No arguments – he's learning,' murmured Moss. 'You're sure about Fenn?'

'I'm sure he vanished from home and there's a .22 rifle missing with him.'

'A pea-shooter,' grunted Moss.

'But still lethal enough if it hits the right spot – and Fenn is army-trained.' Thane prowled the surgery again while he spoke then stooped beside the jagged but intact neck of a smashed liquor bottle. There was a light smear of blood along the glass, broken fragments of the rest lay around. If MacGhee had grabbed the bottle as a weapon and used it, that would account for the cut on his hand. 'Let's hear your story.'

'It isn't much,' shrugged Moss almost apologetically and with a faint embarrassment. 'I – uh – had been going to give Miss Linton . . .'

'Or Margaret . . .' Thane grinned a little.

'I'd been going to give her a lift home,' said Moss determinedly. 'She lives in the village. But she remembered some call she wanted to make first thing tomorrow and she'd left her vet bag in the office. So I drove her out here.' He rubbed a hand across his nose, assembling the facts in the order that mattered. 'The house lights were on and the front door open. I went in first, saw the surgery door open too, then found MacGhee. Then I called you from

97

Margaret's office and after that we took a look around. None of the other rooms seem to have been touched.'

'And the Land-Rover?'

'I hadn't got round to that.' Moss glanced at his watch. 'Eight-thirty now – we got here around eight o'clock. Well, if Fenn took the Land-Rover he's had over half an hour. He could clock up a few miles in that time.'

Thane nodded. 'If he wanted. Margaret Linton didn't leave you at any time?'

'Not till you got here.' Moss scowled. 'Now, look . . .'

'Relax, I only asked,' soothed Thane. He gestured towards the tumbled disorder around. 'Anything taken?'

'She doesn't think so. I didn't let her handle anything:'

They heard a mild, warning cough behind them and turned. Sergeant Imrie guided Margaret Linton into the room then went away.

'You wanted me, Mr Thane?' She came towards them quietly, moving in a careful circle to avoid MacGhee's body. Her mouth showed a trace of fresh lipstick, but her face was still strained and pale.

'For a moment, yes.' Thane glanced around. 'I'm sorry it has to be here, but . . .'

'Blood doesn't worry me,' she assured him steadily, her hands in the pockets of her leather coat. 'If it did, I wouldn't be much good as a veterinary surgeon. And John – well, he was a business partner. It didn't go any deeper. I'm not being callous, just factual.'

'Good.' Thane brought her over and pointed at the knife. 'You're sure that was MacGhee's?'

'Positive. I've seen it often enough. Adam Jennings gave him it as some sort of badge of office in the Children of the Mist.'

'And Jennings was a pretty important client?'

She nodded. 'The kind who pays his bills on the nail.'

'Yes, but . . .' Moss stopped, changed his mind, and shook his head. 'Nothing, Colin.'

Thane gave him a brief, interested glance, got no encour-

98

agement, and went on. 'How genuine was MacGhee about this Home Rule business?'

'Reasonably.' She looked down at her partner's body for a moment and pursed her lips. 'If you mean did it help that Adam Jennings was top of the client list – well, maybe it did. But John put in a lot of work for the Children, unpaid work.'

'Did MacGhee quarrel with Inspector Fenn?'

'Fenn?' Margaret Linton showed no surprise. 'I wondered if – yes, they've had the occasional row. Usually about the Children of the Mist. I wasn't involved, because I've always stayed neutral.' She smiled a little. 'John tried to convert me a couple of times then gave up – I just wasn't interested.'

Thane offered her a cigarette. She took it, accepted a light, and took a slow, deliberate draw on the smoke, waiting, her neat, iron-grey hair glinting in the overhead light. Going over to the window, Thane looked out. The view was to the rear of the house. He could see a torch beam moving among the outhouses as Imrie's men continued their search. But he didn't expect much from there.

'What time should MacGhee have got back here?' he asked, turning.

She shook her head. 'I don't know for sure. Phil and I left at about six.' Moss nodded confirmation, and she went on. 'John had at least a couple of extra cases to visit – they'd come in while he was on his rounds and I'd radioed them on to him.'

Thane had forgotten the radio link to the Land-Rover. 'Where's the set?'

'In my office.'

She led the way out and across the lobby into a smaller version of MacGhee's surgery. Sergeant Imrie was there, still using the telephone. Thane signalled him to carry on and joined Moss and the woman at the compact transmitter cabinet in one corner. Margaret Linton tore the top sheet from a message pad and handed him it.

'These were the late calls – MacDonald and Kenton, both small farmers.'

He passed the message sheet to Moss without comment. They could check it out, get a rough idea of when MacGhee could have arrived back. The radio interested him more. A small red warning light still glowed in one corner and the receiver was humming softly.

Margaret Linton saw his frown and understood. 'I thought I'd put that off,' she confessed wryly. 'But John usually checked to make sure. I've a habit of walking out and forgetting to do it.'

'Better not.' Thane stopped her reaching for the switch. 'Till the fingerprint team are finished, anyway.'

'You mean somebody could have come in here and . . .'

'And called him?' Thane finished it for her and shrugged. 'Any guess is reasonable so far.' He heard Sergeant Imrie hang up and glanced round. 'All fixed, Imrie?'

'Not with Jennings, sir.' Puzzled, Imrie eased a finger round his shirt collar. 'I got through to the farm, an' according to his housekeeper Jennings is on his way here. She said he was bringing some people to see MacGhee.'

'The Children delegation.' Thane swore under his breath at the news. 'What about the Headquarters arrangements?'

'The special search message is going out now,' confirmed the County man. 'They'll have the forensic boys here as soon as they can. But –' he stopped and looked puzzled again – 'they said you'd have company before then anyway, sir. They seemed to think you'd know why.'

'Should I?' Thane raised an inquiring eyebrow in Moss's direction.

Moss regarded him innocently. 'Well, I put the pressure on this afternoon with a certain Assistant Chief Constable . . .'

'About the Marquis?'

'No, the explosives raid caper,' said Moss candidly. 'Sounds like I stirred someone off his backside.'

There was a devil of satisfaction lurking in the untidy, wiry figure's grin and Thane was tempted to learn more. But he fell silent as they heard the growl of a car approaching the house. The engine stopped, there was the sudden slam of a car door and then, a moment later, the rumble of a loud, immediately familiar voice.

'Enter Adam Jennings and his circus,' murmured Moss. 'Will I get rid of them?'

'The way you'd do it would start a local war,' said Thane in a cynical mood. 'Stay here and call Buddha Ilford. Tell him what's happened and that I'm out somewhere.'

'Out?' Moss eyed him with reproach. 'Think he'll believe me?'

'If you try hard enough.' Thane didn't feel like coping with the kind of cross-examination the city C.I.D. chief was likely to throw over the wire. He gave Moss a weary grin of encouragement and left.

Thane was heading down the hall when the house door creaked open to admit a blast of chill night air and a half-frozen County constable. The man came towards him rubbing his hands together in an attempt to coax some warmth into his fingers.

'I've got Adam Jennings outside, sir,' he reported. 'I told him why we're here – he wants to see you.'

'In a moment,' said Thane reluctantly. 'Find anything round the back?'

The constable shook his head then, suddenly, he was pushed aside. Adam Jennings strode angrily into the hallway, ignored the man's grunt of startled protest, and headed straight for Thane.

'Why aren't you out looking for Fenn?' demanded the

dark-haired giant in a harsh rumble, all trace of his usual lazy-moving manner gone. 'If you know he did it . . .'

'Who said so?' Thane threw the constable a flickering glance, saw the man nod apologetically, and swore under his breath. 'All right, we're looking for Fenn. And the rest you already know. John MacGhee's dead. He was stabbed.'

'Then there's trouble ahead,' said Adam Jennings in a bitter, positive voice. 'Thane, this wouldn't have happened if you'd locked up Fenn the way everyone wanted – locked the maniac up instead of wasting time, wasting time because he happened to be one of your own kind.'

'You can go ahead with a speech about it – or you can try to help,' said Thane, refusing to be ruffled. 'Which is it going to be?'

The scowl slowly faded but the anger remained. 'John was a friend. I'll help any way I can.'

Signalling the constable to shut the door, Thane led Adam Jennings towards the surgery. They stopped just inside the room and he gave the man a moment, saying nothing, watching his face. The etched lines of anger didn't change as Jennings looked around.

'Over here.' Thane led the way past John MacGhee's body and stopped again. 'Recognize this knife?'

Adam Jennings squatted down carefully then nodded and rose. 'I should – I gave it to John. The claw setting was specially made, I chose a white and blue stone to represent Scotland's colours.'

Satisfied, Thane beckoned him back to the lobby. Once there, Jennings leaned against the wall, sighed, and ran a hand through his thick hair.

'When did it happen?' he asked grimly.

'Probably an hour ago. We tried to contact you, but you'd already left for here.'

Jennings nodded, his manner moderating a little. 'I promised John I'd bring the Glasgow delegation over – it's the first time they've visited Braedale: I would have

102

been over earlier, but we've been busy. They've been hard at it with me all afternoon.'

'Maybe that was just as well,' mused Thane. He paused for a moment. 'Suppose the man we want is Charlie Fenn. Why would he start here? I'd have placed you at the top of the likely target list.'

'So would I,' snapped Jennings. He pushed himself off the wall. 'But the man is obviously mentally ill. He might have had some fantasy of an idea that he could come here and squeeze something out of John – something which would let him get at me and make people forget about what happened to the Marquis.'

Back to the bull again. Thane fought back a sigh. 'You might be right. What matters is that you'd better not take any chances till we know more. Are your visitors staying?'

'No, they're ready to head home.' Jennings' mouth hardened. 'But don't worry about me. I've a couple of shotguns at the farm – and plenty of friends around.'

They walked back along the lobby. A nod from Thane and the constable opened the door. Outside, Jennings led the way to a cream-coloured station wagon which was drawn up beside the dark shape of the patrol van. The second constable was hovering near and as they approached a small, elderly figure climbed out of the station wagon.

'Adam?' The stranger waited anxiously.

'It's true,' said Jennings shortly. 'I'll tell you later.' He glanced at Thane. 'Chief Inspector, this is Peter Cass, chairman of my Glasgow branch.'

Stoop-shouldered, wearing a heavy overcoat and a black beret with a *skean dhu* brooch, Peter Cass blinked at Thane through a pair of thick spectacles. Behind him the vehicle's two other occupants decided to emerge.

'Eric Francis and Hamilton Campbell,' introduced Jennings briefly, as they came over. 'They're both on our Glasgow rally committee.' He scowled steadily into the

103

night. 'Well, gentlemen, Sunday still goes on as planned. A cause is more important than its individuals.'

It seemed to go down well with the trio. Francis, a longhaired youngster with a University tie, nodded. His companion, an older man with a small, neatly trimmed beard, muttered positive approval.

'You've put a lot of work into it, I suppose,' said Thane neutrally.

'A great deal,' agreed Peter Cass in solemn voice. 'Including today – we've been finalizing details round a table since almost the moment we arrived.'

Jennings gave a brooding grunt. 'Maybe if we'd stopped earlier and come over to see John this wouldn't have happened.' He glanced at Thane, his manner cynical. 'Well, at least the police are reasonably efficient once they finally realize who they're trying to catch.'

Thane rode the insult and stayed unperturbed. 'We do our best,' he said dryly. 'But I'll still send a couple of men along to the farm – just in case.'

'No need.' Jennings sniffed his derision. 'Around here you're the only one who needs help, Thane. Now – and maybe later.'

He signalled to the others and they obediently climbed back into the station wagon. Last aboard, Peter Cass behind the wheel, Jennings nodded a curt goodbye from his window as the engine fired.

The vehicle pulled away. As its tail lights vanished, Thane shrugged and turned to the patiently waiting constable.

'What's your name?'

'MacLaren, sir.' The man came over, shivering.

'Remember what you heard,' said Thane grimly. 'It might just get into the history books some day. It won't do John MacGhee much good, but he just became a ready-made martyr.'

The constable raised a half-interested eyebrow. 'For the Nationalists, you mean?'

Thane shook his head. 'For Adam Jennings – and whatever Jennings wants.' His feet felt like twin blocks of ice and the wind had a knife-like edge. 'Keep an eye open for any more tourists. But better do it from inside the van.'

The constable obeyed thankfully. Thane stayed where he was for a moment longer, his thoughts on Charles Fenn – wherever he might be, whatever he might do next. Then he gave up and strode back into the house.

Margaret Linton's office had a fractionally brighter atmosphere when he returned. The reason was on her desk, an opened bottle of brandy with two used glasses beside it. He noticed Sergeant Imrie trying to keep out of breathing range and could guess why.

'Medicinal aid,' said Moss blandly. 'Personally prescribed for me – and I needed it after speaking to Buddha Ilford.' He grimaced at the memory. 'Our revered Chief Superintendent isn't exactly happy.'

Which was easy enough to understand. Thane watched Margaret Linton pour a fresh tot of brandy into one of the glasses. She brought it over and he downed it gratefully. The warmth of the liquor thawed its way through him and be felt a lot better.

'Did Buddha make any suggestions, Phil?'

'Not the kind I'd like to repeat,' declared Moss wryly. 'But they've traced Sam Hodge's sister – found her living in the Eastern Division.'

It hardly seemed to matter now. But he nodded. 'Any luck with her?'

'None. She hasn't seen or heard from Hodge since his last Christmas card, but isn't too surprised. He's like . . .' Moss' voice died and he swung round, staring at the radio cabinet.

The others had heard it too, a faint scraping noise. It came again, then suddenly, weak and hesitant, a metallic voice came over the receiver.

'Anyone . . . if you can hear, come in. Please come . . . come in. Over.'

'It's him,' said Sergeant Imrie hoarsely, almost unbelievingly. 'Hell, that's Inspector Fenn!'

Three long strides took Thane across the room. He snapped down the switches on the transmitter panel, waiting impatiently for the set to warm.

'Fingerprints,' reminded Moss mildly.

'Stuff them.' Thane scooped up the microphone, scratched a thumb-nail over the fine mesh of the guard, and saw the monitor dial's needle jump.

With a quavering heterodyne squeal as a prelude, Fenn's voice returned again. 'If you can hear, this –' they heard a blend of a groan and a cough – 'this is an emergency call. Come – come in. Over.'

Thane pressed the microphone button. 'Fenn, we read you. This is Thane. Where are you? Over.'

There was almost a minute's tense waiting before the speaker squealed again and Fenn answered.

'Devil's Glen. Repeat, Devil's Glen . . . off the road.' There was another pause and the rasp of heavy breathing. 'Tell – tell Imrie. He'll know. Thane, you – you'll need help. The damned Land-Rover's half on top o' me. Over.'

The voice was fading, either because of the battery power or Fenn's condition. Colin Thane glanced quickly at Sergeant Imrie. The County man nodded he understood.

'All right,' said Thane quickly into the microphone. 'We're coming now. Out.' He put it down. 'Sergeant?'

'He's about six miles north-west o' here,' said Sergeant Imrie, in a flat, precise voice. 'Devil's Glen is the old road up to the snow-line – a sort of slash in the hills wi' the road running through.' He shook his head bleakly. 'If he's gone over, there's a damned long drop with a river at the bottom.'

Behind them, Margaret Linton was already filling her coat pockets with equipment from a cabinet. Without turn-

106

ing, she told them, 'Your nearest doctor is back in the village – but I'll do for a start.'

'Right.' Thane took his decisions quickly. 'Imrie, we'll leave one of your men. He'll arrange an ambulance, towing truck and that doctor, and try to get another couple of men to join him here. You and I lead in the Mini. Phil, you and Margaret follow on with the other constable in the patrol van.'

They headed out at a run.

Sergeant Imrie did the driving. He wasn't patrol car standard but he knew his road, kept his foot hard down, and had a personal urgency to hasten him on. Any last resentment seemed to have gone, replaced by a helpless bewilderment.

'The bloody fool,' he muttered, hands gripping the wheel like twin vices as the Mini tyre-screamed round a bend. 'Ach, maybe Adam Jennings is right – Charlie Fenn has to be off his rocker. Why take the Devil's Glen? Where was he trying to go?'

'Mountains make a good place to hide.' As the little car's headlamps stabbed the dark Thane had a brief glimpse of a heavy truck coming towards them. Then it swept past, with scant inches to spare.

'Main road stuff,' Imrie grunted. 'We turn off – aye, here.' The wheel swung, the Mini tyre-screamed again, they were on a narrow, potholed side road, and he relaxed a little. 'Well, we should have this stretch to ourselves – nobody uses it in winter. But the main road is different. We'd a couple of farmers killed in a crash last month. Both stinking of drink and their pockets crammed with money.'

'Money doesn't seem in short supply around Braedale,' mused Thane. 'Not among the farmers, at any rate.'

'Aye.' Imrie gear-slammed down for a double bend, his lips parting in a humourless grin. 'You know the story about the farmer who wanted a glass partition in his Rolls-

107

Royce?' He broke off to curse as they thumped a pothole and became momentarily airborne. The car slammed down hard, speed undiminished. 'He needed the glass – otherwise the sheep would breathe down his neck all the way to market.'

Thane managed a chuckle.

'Well, it's just a story,' admitted Imrie. 'But I know at least one character around here who brings sacks o' fertilizer home that way.'

'How do vets make out?'

'Fine too.' Imrie changed down quickly for another corner which seemed carved from rising rock and the engine screamed a metallic protest. 'Ach, the only people short o' cash around here are the ones who wear a uniform.'

Which was something Thane had heard before without having to come to Braedale. But he didn't answer, looking ahead, seeing the headlights shining on the start of a white wooden fence which suddenly separated the road from what looked like the start of a sheer drop.

'Devil's Glen,' confirmed Imrie. 'Half a mile o' it. But I can guess where we'll want.'

They kept on, the white fence poles flickering past. Then came a sharp bend, followed by a deceptively angled curve – and halfway along the curve the fence ended in a thirty-foot length of snapped-off stumps. They stopped with their headlamps shining on the gap, Imrie fished a heavy flashlamp from under the dashboard, and they walked over.

The only sounds in the night were the low keening of the wind, an occasional faint crackle from their car's cooling exhaust and a steady murmur of fast, angry water. The County man stopped at the edge, played the flashlamp's powerful beam around, found what he wanted, and brought the light slowly along a downward trail of havoc.

Scrub and gorse had been torn loose, small boulders gouged away, earth scraped bare along that viciously

108

angled path. Then there was a gap of some twenty feet before the havoc continued.

'Bounced,' said Imrie, then made a noise close to a groan as the torchbeam settled on its final target.

The Land-Rover lay like some crumpled toy about two hundred feet below. It had landed on the driver's side to stay that way, stopped precariously in a notch of solid rock, one of the rear wheels missing, most of the cab roof ripped open as if a giant tin-opener had been at work.

And below that notch was the river. A deep, narrow torrent of broken water, mountain water rushing and churning on its way to the lower ground and freedom.

'Damn it to hell,' said Sergeant Imrie in a mixture of despair and disgust. 'Well, we'd better get down.'

Thane glanced round. The patrol van's lights were small twin eyes in the distance, but coming nearer.

'I'll do it,' he said quietly. 'We're going to need a rope at least. You'd better stay here and organize things.'

Sergeant Imrie drew back a step. 'Now look, sir . . .'

'Torch, sergeant.'

He handed it over reluctantly. 'All right. We've a rescue kit in the van. But watch it down there, Chief Inspector. This isn't one o' your city streets.'

Thane grinned, nodded, and started down.

The first stage was easy enough, a heel-digging progression over the broken, rocky slope. But then the going was suddenly steeper, the surface a shifting, small-pebbled channel of gravel-sized rubble which crunched, yielded and vanished from beneath his feet in a series of tiny avalanches. Thane stumbled, lost his balance, almost dropped the torch, twisted to avoid falling headlong, and next moment was skidding down on his back.

That ended when he hit a boulder. The impact knocked most of the breath from his body, but the torch still worked. Panting, shaken, he picked himself up and staggered over a stretch of easier slope towards the smashed vehicle.

'Fenn?' He stopped as he reached the projecting rock, played the torchbeam along the mangled Land-Rover, then moved closer, edging cautiously around the narrow outer ledge very conscious of the rushing water below.

'Over here,' said a faint voice. The torch swung and its light met a blood-stained, haggard face – a face which somehow still managed to force a painful expression of welcome.

But Charles Fenn didn't move. He couldn't. He lay half-under the mangled bodywork, his right leg trapped above the knee between the overturned vehicle and the rock. The passenger door lay nearby, torn from its hinges. The microphone dangled from its cable beside him. How he'd reached it, how the set had operated after that plunge to disaster, were minor miracles.

How he was still alive seemed another.

'You made good time, Thane.' Fenn's voice was little more than a whisper. 'Sorry I can't help – not with this.' He gestured weakly with one hand towards the trapped leg. 'It felt like – like it was broken earlier. Now I'm so damned cold I just can't feel much at all.' He closed his eyes for a moment, breathing heavily from the effort talking had cost him.

'Stay quiet.' Thane edged round beside him, a precarious job with only inches to spare between the end of the spray-damped rock and the downward drop. The chill wind gusted round them and he shivered for a moment as he looked around. They were going to need some kind of leverage to get Fenn free. And it would be tricky. The way the Land-Rover was balanced, too much of a lift could dislodge it completely and send it toppling into the river – probably dragging Fenn with it. Something else had to be considered too. The sharp reek of spilled fuel was strong in his nostrils.

'Thane . . .' Fenn forced himself up a little, using one

110

elbow on the rock and the opposite shoulder against the Land-Rover's metalwork. 'Where is he?'

'Eh?' Thane's main attention had been on the problem of that leg. 'Where's who?'

'MacGhee, man.' It came wearily, impatiently. 'Who – who the hell else?'

Thane frowned hard and swung the torch round. Fenn's blood-streaked face held a strained, puzzled anxiety.

'You mean you don't know?' asked Thane.

Fenn shook his head slightly.

There were people coming down the slope. Thane could hear their feet sliding on the scree channel and the occasional accompanying curse. A couple of torches were flickering towards them.

'Fenn, listen to me,' he said slowly. 'How did you get out here?'

'That – that's something else I don't know.' Fenn gnawed his lip hard, breathing heavily. 'Thane, I – I must have been knocked out. I – damn it, I don't know. Except that I was down here, and my leg hurting like hell.' He winced and moaned a little. 'My leg and my head – and God knows what else. Since maybe half an hour ago.' The breathing grew quicker, the effort taking its toll. 'But this is MacGhee's Land-Rover, right?'

'Yes. And you saw MacGhee earlier. At his house.' The footsteps were almost at the vehicle now. Thane swore to himself, knowing he couldn't stop now. 'Fenn, come on – it matters. What's the last thing you do remember?'

It came as a near mumble, the head starting to loll. 'Went to – went to find out. Then a fight. His . . . his fault. Jumped me.' The mumble trailed away.

'What were you going to find out?' Thane gripped him by the shoulder and shook very gently. 'Charlie, what was it for?'

There was a sigh. The words came low, single, the lips hardly moving. 'Wanted the truth.'

'About the Marquis?'

111

Fenn's headshake was almost imperceptible. 'No. Jennings. About Jennings. More . . . more important.'

Another sigh and the head slumped forward. Then suddenly a slim hand gripped Thane's wrist and pulled it away. Margaret Linton spoke icily from behind him.

'Leave him alone. Haven't you any kind of pity? Or isn't that issued to people like you?'

Thane turned. The woman's face was an angry, tight-lipped mask in the wavering torchlight. Further along the ledge Phil Moss had come to a halt, waiting. It was no time for explanations. He eased back to let her crouch over Fenn, her fury still plain while her small, deft hands moved in a swift examination.

'How bad?' he asked quietly.

'Animals are my province, not this,' she said curtly. 'But he's in pretty poor shape. I'm going to damp down the pain for when he comes round again. Roll up his sleeve.'

Thane did while she fumbled in her pockets. When she edged in there was a small hypodermic in her right hand. The needle went in, she finished the injection, then sank back on her heels.

'That's all – till we get him out.'

They eased back to join Moss. Up above, the patrol van's headlamps glowed beside the Mini and showed the two uniformed figures floundering down towards them. Sergeant Imrie arrived first, a compact lifting jack cradled in his arms. The constable followed, equally laden with items from the patrol van's rescue kit.

Setting the lifting jack down, Imrie gave a grunt of relief then considered the overturned Land-Rover gloomily.

'We'd be best to wait for the tow-truck,' he declared after a minute. 'It could give us some kind o' an anchor from up top. The way that thing's balanced . . .' He shook his head.

'He won't last long as he is,' said Margaret Linton

bluntly. 'Pulse and respiration are poor. We need to win time, not waste it.'

'Like that, eh?' Imrie scrubbed his chin. 'MacLaren . . .'

'Sarge?' The constable dumped his share of the rescue gear and came nearer.

'We'll have a try, lad. No flares –' Imrie sniffed the fuel-heavy air – 'otherwise we could blow ourselves to Hell an' back. Spikes in the rock higher up, then we'll rope her fore and aft.' He glanced at the others. 'We'll need some help wi' the torches.'

They took on the job of lamp-holding while the two County men set to work. MacLaren used a trio of ring-ended piton-style spikes, slightly thicker than the mountaineering variety. Spacing them carefully, he hammered them into cracks in the rock above the Land-Rover and kept an old rag between hammer and spike to cut down the risk of sparks. By the time he'd finished Sergeant Imrie had one end of the nylon rope secured near the rear of the vehicle's chassis. He scrambled up, fed the rope through the ring-ends, went down again, and tied the remaining end to the front axle.

A last check to make sure there was no slack on the rope, then he picked up the jack.

'Sir.' He turned to Thane. 'If you and Inspector Moss will get him clear I'll stay on the jack. If anything goes wrong, we get out fast.'

Thane nodded. Moss contented himself with a grunt.

They inched round the tiny outer ledge, Sergeant Imrie in the lead, the rushing water loud below. In the open beyond, Margaret Linton and MacLaren positioned themselves one on either side of the vehicle, shining the torch-beams for maximum effect.

Fenn was still lying as they'd left him. Which, decided Thane, was probably as well. An unconscious man felt no pain and those few moments getting him clear – he pushed the possibilities aside, watching Imrie.

It took a couple of minutes for that crouching figure to

find a spot where he could get enough clearance between the Land-Rover and the rock to allow the jack to slip into position. Then, still in a crouch, he began to work the stub handle in a slow rhythm. The jack rose, bit into the metal and gradually, creaking in protest, the vehicle began to rise.

One inch . . . two . . . the bodywork gave a shudder, started to lurch, then steadied as the rope suddenly tautened. Thane swallowed hard then Imrie nodded and began working the handle again.

'Nearly there,' said Moss sharply. 'Another inch.'

'Right.' Imrie pumped again.

There was a sudden metallic twang. A twang which heralded an immediate shudder as the Land-Rover's tail began to slide in a slow, downward metal-scraping path towards the edge.

'Spike's gone.' Sergeant Imrie hauled himself upright, despair on his face. 'Out. Quick, both o' you.'

Thane's reflexes took him two stumbling steps towards safety. Then he stopped. There was a tiny spur of rock projecting just ahead. Enough for a footgrip. And the sliding, grumbling tail of the Land-Rover was just above.

A half-turn and his left foot was jammed against the spur. He reached up, spreading his arms, hands meeting the metal. Teeth clenched hard, he took the strain as the downward movement continued – took the strain and managed to hold it, desperately maintaining that vital balance.

Behind him, Phil Moss swore incredulously then swung back.

'Keep the jack going,' shouted Moss. 'Hurry it up, sergeant.'

The low, pumping clack of the little handle began again. The Land-Rover kept rising, a fraction of an inch each clack – and with each fraction the pressure on Thane's arms seemed to grow. Sweat ran down his face, an agoniz-

114

ing quiver began to run across his shoulders and down towards his legs.

'We're almost there, Colin.' Moss's voice, pitched high and tense, held a desperate encouragement. 'Keep it like that – keep it.'

Thane couldn't answer, couldn't even nod. The world had shrunk until it only consisted of his hands, his arms and that terrible weight above. The quivering across his shoulders was increasing, each new second seemed the last he could possibly fight against that pressure.

There was a hurried, dragging rustle along the ledge, heading towards the front of the Land-Rover.

'He's out,' yelled Moss a moment later. 'We're clear. Now you, Colin – and fast. She's going.'

Thane took a deep, shuddering breath then another. Then he dropped his arms and stumbled to the side, sensing the vehicle beginning to lurch as he went. Next moment Constable MacLaren had caught him and dragged him clear.

Nothing could stop the Land-Rover's final grinding, shuddering slide. The tail left the rock first, leaving the battered front end suspended by the rope. For a long minute it hung there like some dead pendulum weight. Then the two remaining spikes above were dragged loose by the constant strain.

The vehicle vanished. A heavy splash came from the darkness below and spray rose high to patter around them. As the splash died the river resumed its angry, rushing song.

'You bloody fool,' said Phil Moss with a shaky dignity. 'You complete bloody fool. Headquarters would have skinned me if I'd brought you back dead.'

Thane managed a wobbling grin and sat down fast, wondering if the ache in his arms and the trembling in his body would ever cease. A few yards away, he could see Margaret Linton easing a blanket round the limp but living outline that was Inspector Charles Rennie Fenn.

115

Who might or might not be guilty of murder.

A hand touched his shoulder and he looked round. Sergeant Imrie was there, a lip-biting Constable MacLaren a pace or two to the rear. 'About that spike, the one that came loose –' Imrie grimaced – 'I'm sorry. MacLaren tried it, I tried it . . .'

Thane shook his head, dismissing the matter. More headlights were coming along the Devil's Glen road, the ambulance and another car.

'Where will they take him, sergeant?'

'The cottage hospital at Pitlochry's about nearest,' said Imrie. He hesitated then asked diffidently, 'Did you – well, did you get a chance to ask him, sir?'

'About MacGhee?' Thane nodded. 'A little. He says he doesn't know.'

'You mean he's lost his memory?' asked Imrie cautiously.

Thane shrugged. That was one he wasn't going to answer – not yet. 'Take over here,' he ordered, getting shakily to his feet. 'I'm borrowing the Mini and heading back.'

'To the village?' Imrie nodded a careful understanding. 'Somebody should, I think. We'd a call on the van radio before we brought the gear down. There's only one man at the station, and he was getting anxious about something or other – I didn't take time to find out.'

'We'll check,' said Thane.

Moss joined him and they started the steep climb together. Halfway up they met the ambulance crew coming down with a stretcher, a tall man with a doctor's bag fussing alongside. On the road, a squat tow-truck was just pulling in behind the other vehicles. The truck's engine died, the driver's door opened, and Dave Anderson climbed out.

He saw them and came straight over. 'How bad is it?'

'Down there?' Phil Moss considered briefly. 'Well, you

could say we almost got our feet wet.' He grinned at Anderson then followed Thane aboard the Mini.

Twenty minutes later they drove into Braedale village and turned towards the police station. As the building's lights appeared ahead Thane pursed his lips in a silent whistle and slowed.

The street outside was almost filled with silent figures. Young figures, youths and girls, some armed with heavy sticks, others holding a variety of makeshift weapons, here and there the ominous line of a shotgun barrel, they were waiting with a steady, uncanny patience – and he could guess why.

A way parted for the Mini as it came nearer. He stopped it outside the station door, climbed out and made a rough count while Moss came round to join him. There were between forty and fifty youngsters in the crowd. Youngsters who met his gaze in absolute silence.

'Inside, Phil,' he said quietly.

They didn't get that far. The door opened and Adam Jennings stalked out, a worried-looking County constable trailing at his heels.

'We're ready, Thane,' said Jennings bleakly. He had a shotgun slung over one shoulder.

'Ready?' Thane raised a weary eyebrow. 'For what?'

Jennings growled under his breath and drew himself erect, chest swelling. 'To help you search for Fenn.' An arm waved briefly towards their intent audience. 'John MacGhee was one of us. The Children of the Mist demand the right to help find the man who murdered him.'

It was a long time since Thane had felt such a wave of instant anger. He glanced past Jennings to the constable, who shook his head.

'I told them to get home, sir. And that you'd already found the inspector . . .'

'If you have, where is he?' demanded Jennings loudly.

'On his way to hospital.' Thane's voice was cold as

117

crushed ice. 'More dead than alive, if it interests you. Jennings, I'll give you five minutes to get every one of your tame vigilantes out of here. After that, if I see anyone with as much as a toy pistol around here –' he stopped and deliberately prodded Jennings on the chest – 'you personally get thrown in a cell.'

He gestured Moss and the County man to follow, led the way into the station building, and slammed the door once they'd entered. It closed on a rising hubbub of voices.

'Sorry, sir,' said the constable greyly.

'Forget it,' Thane told him, grimly philosophical. 'Adam Jennings loves a chance to grandstand. This was made to order for him. What else has been happening?'

'Not much, sir. Glasgow called a couple of times trying to contact you. But they said it could wait. And Detective Inspector Elliot arrived from County Headquarters – he's at MacGhee's place now.'

'That's the man,' said Moss with a grin of satisfaction. 'Elliot handled the armoury raid job.'

'Then we'd better see him,' said Thane almost reluctantly. He glanced at the constable. 'Can you raise an extra car from somewhere?'

'Yes, easy enough.'

'Get it, collect Mrs Fenn and her daughter, and take them to Pitlochry hospital.'

'I . . .' The constable hesitated, shoved his peaked cap back a little on his forehead, and looked worried again. 'Well, I'm on my own here. If I go the station will be empty.'

'So who's going to steal it?' growled Moss. 'We'll send someone back from the bungalow. Now get moving.'

The constable obeyed. When they followed him out, the street was empty. But a large *skean dhu* symbol had been chalked in white opposite the doorway.

From bravado – or as a warning?

Thane wished he knew which.

Chapter Six

Detective Inspector Jonas Elliot might be newly arrived. But for a man who came to have a more or less friendly chat only to find a brand-new murder part of the deal, he was already well briefed.

They found him waiting in John MacGhee's surgery, a plump, sparse-haired individual with a weather-beaten tan and a slight limp. He shook hands affably with Thane and grinned at Moss.

'I've talked to the constables and I made a couple of calls to County Headquarters,' said Elliot easily. 'Our finger-print boys should arrive from Perth within the hour, but the medical examiner side isn't so easy. You grabbed Brae-dale's only doctor for Charlie Fenn. I'm not complaining, but it means that side will have to wait till he gets back or until a tame medic Headquarters are sending manages to get here.' He stuck his hands in the pockets of his brown pin-stripe suit, an action which emphasized a well-nurtured paunch. 'Did you get much out of Fenn?'

'A little. Not much more than that he came here.' Thane looked around the surgery. Someone had draped a sheet over MacGhee's body, otherwise the scene was unchanged.

'I did that,' said Elliot in a mild apology. 'Looks more decent, I think. Well, now I'm here who does what?'

'Protocol?' Thane raised a cautious eyebrow. County C.I.D. officers could be either stubborn or co-operative, depending on how they viewed intruders in their territory.

119

He wasn't too sure which category D.I. Elliot would match.

'Just keeping my nose clean,' assured Elliot with a phlegmatic calm. 'I know Charlie Fenn started off as your special pigeon. I don't mind him staying that way provided country lads like myself get – ah . . .'

'Their share of the action?' queried Moss dryly. 'I'd say there's enough to go round.'

Thane nodded agreement.

'Fine.' Elliot brightened. 'That's how my bosses want it. So where do we start?'

'By sending one of the uniform men back to hold the fort at Braedale.' Thane left them for a moment, detailed one of the trio of constables outside the room to head back, then returned. 'Elliot, do you know Charlie Fenn?'

'Uh-huh.' Elliot gave a slightly doleful shrug. 'I've worked with him a couple of times, but never on anything big. We – well, we rubbed along. I wouldn't say more.' He nodded towards the sheet on the floor. 'Except that I wouldn't have figured on this. Apart from the obvious, does it link in with the Marquis?'

'Not according to Fenn.' Thane told him what little the injured man had said and saw the County detective blink.

'Jennings?' Elliot shook his head. 'Well, I suppose I might have guessed. Fenn threw that name at me often enough when I had the armoury raid on my plate.' He treated Moss to a fairly chilly glance. 'Which brings me to why I came anyway. Why stir that thing up again?'

Moss gave a thin-shouldered shrug and showed no sign of repentance. 'You didn't make any arrests.'

'No.' Elliot scowled a little.

'And none of the demolition charges have ever turned up,' reminded Moss. 'Four whole cases of nitrostarch, vanished. If your theory about a safe-blowing mob was right . . .'

'Was right?' D.I. Elliot swallowed hard. 'Look, it has to

be right. The bunch that pulled the Dunkeld raid gave us only two leads, but both of them pointed straight at Glasgow, your territory. They dropped a pair of brand-new wire cutters when they went through the fence – expensive cutters, traced back to one of the biggest hardware stores in Glasgow. We found tyre tracks near the fence and a van was spotted driving away. The same van was abandoned outside Glasgow early the next morning – rented from a firm in the city by a character who used a phoney name and a faked driving licence.'

'You're sure it was the same van?' queried Thane mildly, trying to stay neutral.

'Glasgow Scientific Bureau said so,' declared Elliot triumphantly. 'They matched our tyre tracks against the van's treads.'

Moss winced but went on doggedly. 'Did you run a check on Jennings?'

Elliot sighed. 'Eventually. To keep Fenn quiet, no other reason. Damn it, Adam Jennings has the most copperbottomed alibi of all time – he was in Glasgow when the raid happened, taking part in a TV discussion show.' He smiled faintly. 'And before you ask, it was a live show. How do you get round that one?'

'We don't,' said Thane quickly, scenting trouble if he let the fencing continue. 'We get some work done.' He gestured towards the toppled filing cabinet and its spilled papers. 'There's a start. I want any records on the Marquis, any correspondence with Jennings, anything else that looks interesting.'

He left Moss and Elliot to mutter over the task and tackled the unpleasant business of going through John MacGhee's pockets. They yielded a surprisingly small harvest – a bunch of keys, a blood-stained wallet with some credit cards and a few pounds in money, a part-used veterinary prescription pad and a small pocket appointment diary formed the final collection. Replacing the

121

sheet, he looked round to see how his companions were getting on.

'So far just these,' said Moss, thumbing towards a thin bundle of papers on the floor. 'Elliot?'

D.I. Elliot shrugged from the other side of the room. 'Not much. This cupboard is locked.'

Thane tossed him the keys. One opened the cupboard. Elliot rummaged inside briefly then shook his head.

'Animal medicines, mostly.' He stopped, brightening, as he heard the sound of a car drawing up. 'This should be our fingerprint squad.'

It was. Three men, headed by a sergeant, brought in the tools of their trade – camera and portable photo-lights, powder sprays and brushes, the inevitable plastic collecting bags and the rest. It was a time when any non-specialist cop knew it was wise to move clear.

Thane collected the bundle of papers and led the way out. They were in the corridor, a bright glare of lights already shining from the surgery, when the bungalow's main door swung open. The tall, slightly built doctor whom Thane had seen at Devil's Glen came in out of the cold swearing mildly and rubbing his hands.

Elliot knew him and grinned a welcome. 'Hello, Doctor Cairns. Busy night.'

'For some of us,' said the medical man brusquely. He nodded as Elliot completed the introductions. 'Pity I missed your strong-man act back there, Chief Inspector. If you wake up tomorrow with a pain in your back you'll know you've slipped a disc.'

Thane's mouth twitched at the corners. 'I'll remember. How's Fenn?'

Cairns shrugged. 'Clinical diagnosis by torchlight isn't my strong point. But I'd say there's a badly crushed leg, smashed ribs, and the chance of a query fractured skull. He won't do any running away.'

'But he'll live?' asked Thane patiently.

'He should. Margaret Linton volunteered to go in the

ambulance with him and I told her she was welcome. Oh, and Sergeant Imrie said to tell you he'd gone along too.' He glanced towards the surgery. 'In there?'

Elliot nodded. 'Yes, but . . .'

'It shouldn't take long.' The doctor strode past them and through the doorway. They heard briefly raised voices then silence.

'He doesn't waste time,' murmured Phil Moss.

'With his size of practice he can't,' said Elliot. He grimaced. 'I saw him do a post mortem once – strictly mad axeman style. But he knows his stuff.'

They were smoking cigarettes in Margaret Linton's room when Cairns finally returned, buttoning his coat again.

'I've got all you'll need for now,' he said briefly. 'Time of death around 7.30 p.m. – that's on body temperature and a touch of rigor around the eyelids, but remember I'm approximating. Cause of death was the wound in his throat. It went through the jugular vein, of course. No other injuries that mattered a twopenny damn.' He yawned, a tired man. 'The rest will keep for your own people, I imagine. They can contact me if I'm needed. Good night.'

He turned on his heel and marched off.

'Jugular vein, of course,' mimicked Moss. He scratched one ear and turned to Thane. 'The same time of death, though – we've still to find out when MacGhee probably got back.'

Thane brought out the names he'd been given by Margaret Linton and glanced at Elliot.

'I'll do it,' nodded the County detective. 'I can phone from here. And I don't mind staying on if you want – the fingerprint bunch won't rush things.'

As ideas went, it seemed better than most. They left Elliot deciding which was the most comfortable chair and headed out.

It was close on midnight as Thane drove the Mini back

through a sleeping, silent Braedale towards the police station. At his side, Moss scowled as they purred along the deserted village street.

'What do you think?' he demanded suddenly.

'About Fenn?' Thane shrugged. 'The pattern seems simple enough, Phil. He walks out to the bungalow, starts talking with MacGhee. Then a quarrel, a fight, MacGhee grabs the bottle, Fenn sees the knife . . .'

'Just like that?'

He wondered himself. On an impulse he knocked the car out of gear as they neared the police station and let it coast into the kerb. They stopped outside Fenn's house.

'There's nobody home,' reminded Moss dryly. 'And we haven't got a warrant.'

'Then we're just making sure the property's secure,' suggested Thane affably. 'We should, now there's no constable to spare to keep an eye on the place.'

'Which is just as well.' Moss sighed, followed him out of the car, and felt for the little piece of flexible plastic he habitually kept in his handkerchief pocket. Cops and their families usually locked doors, whatever the local custom. 'Front or back?'

'Back. Less chance of an audience.'

They went round quietly, walking along a grass border, enough moonlight filtering through the clouds to let them see and avoid the hazard of a line of staked plants.

Then, almost simultaneously, they stopped short.

The back door was already open, almost to its full width. They could see a faint glow of light coming from somewhere inside.

'Phil . . .' It came from Thane as a murmur and he made a brief circling motion with one hand. Moss nodded, knowing the drill. Only an amateur was likely to try to escape the same way he'd come in. He swung round and padded off again towards the front.

Thane gave him a ten-second count then made his own move. Half a dozen swift, animal-quiet steps brought him

124

to the opened door. It hadn't been forced. The cylinder lock was a simple rim-edge affair any thin-bladed knife could have eased back. Lips shaping a thin, silent whistle, Thane slipped through into a small, neat kitchen. He stopped again, looking around, every sense alert. The soft glow of light was coming from a room off the hallway just beyond, a room with its door fractionally ajar. As he waited there was the faint wood-against-wood murmur of a drawer being opened.

Tip-toeing forward, he reached the door. There was a bedroom beyond. He could see that much, and the shadow of a crouching figure cast on the nearest wall. The shadow moved and another drawer murmured.

Gently, Thane eased the door wider. It squeaked – loud and clear. And, throwing caution aside, he went in fast.

A torch was lying on the carpeted floor beside a small bureau which had one drawer still open. And the dark silhouette of a man was swinging round from beside it, rising from a crouch in a strange floor-clawing movement. Sheer bad luck meant there was a double bed like a barrier between them. Sheer good luck made Thane stumble against it and almost lose his balance – at the same time as the gun now in the intruder's hand swung up and slammed a wild, orange-tongued shot in his direction.

The bullet hit the wall behind him, ricocheting. There was a smash of breaking glass. But by then Thane had hit the floor beside the shelter of the bed, rolling, hugging desperately for cover. Another shot barked, the lead burying itself deep in the bedding just above his head.

There was a sudden cold draught of air, a grunt, a rustle of movement, then, as he tensed, a soft thud. And almost in unison the front door of the house had been slammed back on its hinges and someone was running towards the room from down the hall.

A moment later the room light clicked on. Phil Moss peered in cautiously then relief showed on his face as Thane rose slowly to his feet.

'What the hell were you doing down there?' he demanded.

'Trying to be an ostrich,' said Thane with a heavy sarcasm.

The room was empty, the draught came from a flapping curtain and the large opened window behind it. Thane went over and peered into the night. Nothing moved out there. Their quarry's escape route had been well planned – but not along the line they'd expected. He turned, then saw both gun and torch lying near the bed.

'Would you know him again?' asked Moss hopefully.

'No – not a chance.' Thane stooped and picked the gun up carefully by the barrel. He'd already known what it had to be – a British Service issue .38 Webley revolver, the smell of freshly burned cordite still clinging to the metal. Moss watching, he broke it open and checked the cylinder.

Three cartridges had been fired, three still remained.

'Think it's the same one?' queried Moss.

'I'd bet on it.' Thane paused for a long moment. 'Well, which was it, Phil? Was he trying to get the gun out of here – or planning to leave it for us to find?'

Moss shook his head in puzzled indecision, collected the abandoned torch in a handkerchief, then glanced around. The first bullet's ricochet had smashed a dressing table mirror. The second was going to take some digging to recover from the mattress. He waited while Thane examined the bureau drawers. They held Inspector Fenn's spare shirts and underclothing.

Shrugging, Thane closed the window. Then they closed the front and back doors and drove the Mini the rest of the way to the police station.

They parked outside and were walking into the building when Moss gave a sudden grunt and nudged. A big, regally old-fashioned Daimler limousine was drawn in at the far side of the station, half-hidden by a parked patrol van. Thane whistled his surprise. To any cop from Glasgow the Daimler was an unmistakable trademark. But he

126

shook his head at Moss's silent, questioning glance and they went in.

The Daimler's owner was waiting in Fenn's office, perched somewhat impatiently on a chair. Another surprise in the shape of Constable Copeland stood awkwardly by his side.

'Far from the madding crowd, eh, Chief Inspector?' A gaunt, bony figure with a lined, skull-tight face which seemed to crack as the lips moved, Professor Andrew MacMaster held the Regius chair of Forensic Medicine at Glasgow University – which in the mind-scorched humour of generations of students made him a connoisseur on all things dead or damnable. He gave Moss a more or less amiable nod and went on, 'I was invited to participate in the MacGhee affair, at my usual scale fee of course.'

Thane murmured his understanding. The elderly University expert could and did work for whom he pleased, impartial scientific investigation as his stock in trade.

'Ilford called me,' explained MacMaster. His long, thin fingers fanned sadly. 'Awkwardly enough, I had friends in for a rubber of bridge – but as he said the County force were particularly anxious, it was duty before pleasure.'

'We can certainly use you,' admitted Thane, peeling off his coat and hanging it up.

'That much I'd gathered,' murmured MacMaster. He smiled almost benignly towards Copeland. 'As this young fellow required transport I brought him with me. He was able to supply some quite – ah – useful background on the way.'

Phil Moss grunted, wondering how useful. 'Everything done as we wanted, Copeland?'

'Yes, sir.' Constable Copeland nodded solemnly. 'Inspector Fenn's car and clothes delivered to the Scientific Branch – I've the official receipt from a Superintendent Laurence.'

Professor MacMaster sniffed at the name. He and Dan Laurence frequently found their territories overlapping –

127

and fought like cat and dog when it happened. Understanding, grinning a little, Thane came over.

'How about the photo-copy stuff from Records?' he demanded.

'On the desk, sir.' Copeland gestured towards an envelope. 'But – well, it doesn't seem to matter much now, does it?' His young, broken-nosed face flushed. 'I mean . . .'

'I know what you mean.' Thane's grin faded and he tossed the Mini's ignition key on the desk. 'So you can get straight back to work. There's a gun and torch lying in the outer office. Take them down to the fingerprint mob at MacGhee's bungalow and say I want them checked. And later they've to check Fenn's house.'

He told Copeland why, with MacMaster an interested audience. Then, as he finished, he glanced at the forensic expert. 'Professor, we'll need a comparison test on the gun and bullets – including the bullet from the Marquis.'

'Which I can do without any need to involve County people or Laurence's band of uncouth guerrillas,' said MacMaster crisply. 'But first I'd like to see my – ah – cadaver. If Copeland's driving out there I can follow him along.'

'The local doctor had a look at MacGhee,' volunteered Moss. 'He reckons time of death was around seven-thirty.'

'No doubt he did his best.' MacMaster showed a minimal interest. 'However, I prefer to start from scratch. And once I can have the body moved –' he stopped and frowned – 'there are mortuary facilities, I suppose?'

Thane glanced at Copeland. The County constable nodded. 'We've a wee place at the back here, sir. But – well, we usually store found property in it.'

MacMaster sighed and closed his eyes briefly. 'Then have it cleaned out, man. I have no wish to spend the night surrounded by abandoned debris.'

Copeland swallowed and muttered he'd get it done. They went out and after a moment the sound of the Mini starting up was followed by the throaty purr of the Daimler's engine.

'He's a rat-faced old devil,' growled Moss as the sound of the cars pulling away began to fade. 'Still, now . . .'

He didn't have to finish. They both knew that Mac-Master, however difficult he might be to deal with, happened to be undisputed top of his league. Thane lit a cigarette, dropped wearily into the chair behind Fenn's desk, and opened the Records Office envelope. It contained three individual photo-copy sheets.

He glanced at them almost casually then suddenly sat bolt upright and swore in something very close to disbelief.

'What's up?' queried Moss, amused. 'Got the wrong cards from them?'

There was no answering smile on Thane's face. Wordlessly, he handed Moss one of the sheets. It had the usual C.R.O. layout, the name 'Thomas Dougan' and full-face and profile photographs which were unmistakably the blond, scarred head cattleman.

'Previous convictions,' said Thane bitterly. 'Read them, Phil.'

There were five. The first two were for petty theft. The third was for attempted safe-blowing, the fourth for possession of explosives, the fifth . . .

Moss carefully moistened his lips. 'A parcel-bomb job – but . . .'

'Six years for it, and he's been out for three years since,' nodded Thane slowly. 'An English case, otherwise we might have heard about it.' He sighed and stared almost viciously at the ceiling. 'Well, you wanted a link between Adam Jennings and explosives.'

'Uh-huh.' Moss scowled to himself. 'If Fenn had . . .'

'Checked?' Thane shook his head. 'Charlie Fenn was too interested in Jennings to get down to bothering about the hired help.' He sat silent for a moment, the cigarette burning unheeded, his mind struggling to achieve some kind of

129

order out of the growing confusion. 'Jennings has his Home Rule rally in Glasgow on Sunday night.'

'With maybe a bomb as a curtain-raiser?' Moss considered the prospect calmly. 'It would make good publicity – if he was careful enough.'

But their worry was still supposed to be MacGhee's murder. MacGhee's murder and Inspector Charles Rennie Fenn. With that damned bull still perhaps holding the basic answers. Thane clenched his fists and stared at the ceiling. Then he sighed.

'You made those background checks?'

'Like you asked.' Moss sat on the edge of the desk, his legs swinging. 'All I found out about the Fenn family is that he has always had a temper, that his wife holds the balance and that the girl used to work as a secretary till she got fired.'

'For?'

Moss grinned. 'Telling the boss where to put his typewriter. It's a family failing.'

Thane nodded ruefully. 'And the row between Sam Hodge and Jennings?'

'Hodge seems an argumentative old cuss but he liked his job – or seemed to.' Moss slipped a bismuth tablet into his mouth and sucked for a moment. 'There's a story around that Adam Jennings fired him simply to cut down the wage bill. That might make sense – Jennings is pretty tight for cash.'

Thane showed his surprise. 'He pays his bills.'

'Around here,' agreed Moss. 'Not outside Braedale. I phoned a pal of mine in one of the credit rating outfits. Jennings couldn't raise a rating good enough to buy a pair of socks by instalments. As far as I can figure it, he spent too much money on that damned castle – and a lot of the Children of the Mist campaign money comes out of his own pocket. I'll bet his bank overdraft would give you nightmares.'

'Then getting 120,000 dollars for the Marquis . . .'

130

'Must have looked like manna from Texas,' concurred Moss. 'Well, at least he still gets a fair whack from the insurance. But whoever shot the Marquis really did hit him where it hurts.'

'You said whoever . . .'

'I know.' Moss grinned. 'Think it could have been Sam Hodge who was at Fenn's place?'

'If it was, we didn't get to the conversational stage,' Thane said sardonically. 'He can wait.'

They turned with a mutual reluctance to the files they'd brought from MacGhee's surgery. Going through them was a slow, wearisome task – but it had to be done. MacGhee's veterinary records on the bull, his correspondence with Adam Jennings both professional and on Children of the Mist business seemed straightforward and uniformly dull.

There was a tap on the door and they broke off, glad of any interruption. Sergeant Imrie entered and clicked his heels with a touch of formality.

'Reporting back from the hospital, sir.'

They grinned. The County man was in his shirt sleeves with his tie hanging loose and carpet slippers on his feet. He carried a mug of coffee in each hand.

'You're improperly dressed, sergeant,' said Thane mildly. 'Congratulations.'

'Aye.' Imrie yawned despite himself and placed the mugs in front of him. 'I thought you could use these – it's damned nearly 2 a.m.'

Thane glanced at his watch in some surprise then sipped the coffee thankfully. 'How was Charlie Fenn when you left?'

Sergeant Imrie took a deep breath and shook his head. 'They've had him in theatre, sir. According to the surgeon they'll probably save the leg. But he'll need more surgery before they're sure.'

'Has his wife seen him?'

'And the girl,' nodded Imrie. 'But he's going to be

131

sleeping off the anaesthetic for a good few hours. The Pitlochry police have a couple o' men there, just in case. So I came back – I thought I'd maybe do more good here.'

The telephone rang. Moss scooped it up, answered, then covered the mouthpiece. 'Elliot, from MacGhee's place. You want to take it?'

Thane waved a negative hand and waited. Moss held a brief conversation with the County man then hung up, his face far from happy.

'Well?' queried Thane.

'Interim report,' said Moss dryly. 'They've found finger-prints on that *skean dhu* thing, but no prints on the gun, no prints on the torch. And Elliot says Professor MacMaster is going around chortling like a kid at a picnic over that stab wound and saying how glad he is he came.'

Thane groaned with a sense of dull foreboding. 'Any idea why?'

'None.'

'That's it, then.' Thane rubbed his hands across his eyes, knowing there was only one sensible thing remaining. 'We'll get some sleep, Phil – and you too, sergeant. Leave word for Elliot and MacMaster that I want an 11 a.m. conference.' He saw Imrie's eyebrows rising and grinned wearily. 'Don't worry, sergeant. We won't be idle all that time.'

Which was bad news for Moss.

Braedale had a thin drizzle of sleet and snow before dawn. It swept in from the mountains, lasted for about an hour, then died.

And the sun came up, bright, mildly warming in a suddenly cloudless sky, chasing the last traces of frosted white, holding its own reminder of a spring not too far ahead.

It shone on a village where more people than usual stopped to gossip when they met. It shone on a cluster of parked, travel-stained press cars and the sharp-eyed, casually dressed strangers who'd arrived in them before dawn. They were the vanguard, a handful of reporters and photographers who watched each coming and going from the police station with apparent disinterest but who could have recited every detail with timetable accuracy.

Across the road from the station stood four teenagers. There had been four there since dawn – the number stayed constant though from time to time the faces changed as they were relieved by others.

The Children of the Mist were holding their own kind of vigil. They'd been photographed, interviewed, and now from the press point of view could be ignored.

Colin Thane made his official arrival minutes before 11 a.m. . . . though he'd been at the station twice already since seven-thirty, using a back door and a short-cut through Sergeant Imrie's vegetable garden.

He smiled a little and nodded to the patiently waiting pressmen, knowing most of them, liking a few, being prepared to tolerate the rest. He let the photographers move in, halted briefly for their clicking shutters, then it was the notebook squad's turn.

'A straight question,' said a dark, wiry, long-nosed individual in the forefront. 'Has Fenn been charged, Chief Inspector?'

'Straight answer – no.' Thane rubbed a hand along his jawline. 'Didn't you get a statement from Detective Inspector Elliot?'

'Full of pace and drama,' nodded the reporter cynically. 'He needs a new scriptwriter.'

Thane fought down a chuckle. For practical reasons he believed in good press relations. Publicity could either help or hinder an investigation – it depended how you managed to shape it, how far the pressmen would go along with you. That meant the kind of co-operation which was as fragile as an eggshell. But if you were careful it wouldn't be broken too often.

'Take a drive along to Devil's Glen about noon,' he told

133

them casually. 'We're planning to fish the Land-Rover out of the river.' He let the murmur of interest die down. 'Now it's my turn. Who tipped off the news desks that we'd a murder?'

If it had been a cop – and that happened – he wouldn't get an answer. Wouldn't expect it.

The long-nosed reporter glanced at the others and drew a series of fractional nods. He shrugged. 'Adam Jennings – you know the song. Every cloud has its silver lining and this one could help drum up interest for his Home Rule wardance.'

Thane didn't comment, left them, and went into the station office. Freshly shaven, uniform newly pressed, Sergeant Imrie was waiting inside the door.

'Everyone here?' asked Thane briefly.

'Still waiting on the Professor, sir,' reported Imrie. 'He said he'd be back in time.' He came nearer, frowning a little. 'Eh . . . about last night, sir. I was having a talk with the men about – well, what happened. There's a thing I don't understand.'

'I've a whole list of them,' murmured Thane. 'Go on.'

'It's about Adam Jennings.' Imrie paused uncertainly, noting Thane's suspicious glance. 'This is on pure fact, nothing else. Did he say those visitors of his were in Braedale for the first time?'

Thane nodded, wondering what was coming.

'One of the constables got the station wagon's registration number,' said Imrie quietly. 'He was certain he'd seen it before, and he was right. We've got it on the car lists for those committee meetings at the farm, sir. Three times in the last two months. I remember checking the number with Motor Taxation – it belongs to a Peter Cass.'

For a moment Thane said nothing, thinking of the small man with a Children of the Mist badge on his beret. Jennings had lied – a small lie, perhaps. But small lies could sometimes have big reasons.

'I'll keep it in mind,' he said slowly then saw Mac-

Master coming into the building. 'Make sure we're not disturbed.'

Imrie gave a resolute nod and faded away. MacMaster cheerfully at his heels, Thane went through to Fenn's tiny office. Phil Moss was already there with a somewhat weary-looking Detective Inspector Elliot.

'All present, eh?' MacMaster rubbed his thin, bony hands together virtuously. 'I've been for a short walk – make the most of any out-of-town jaunts, that's my motto.'

Moss grunted. Jonas Elliot watched bleakly as the elderly forensic expert took a seat.

'Let's get started,' said Thane, taking up position behind the desk. 'Phil, what's the latest report on Fenn?'

'Out of danger.' Moss doodled idly with a pencil on the notebook which rested on his lap. 'I phoned the hospital ten minutes ago. But he's still under sedation.'

'Right.' Thane turned to Elliot. 'And the general situation?'

The County detective leaned forward, welcoming the opportunity. 'I checked MacGhee's last few farm visits. He probably got home about six-thirty. If the seven-thirty time of death is near enough to accurate –' he glanced at Mac-Master and received a fractional nod – 'then we've got the beginnings of a timetable.'

'Fingerprints?'

'Enough,' agreed Elliot grimly. 'We collected a set from Fenn early this morning – though the hospital didn't exactly approve. They match the prints on that knife and plenty of others around the surgery. We found MacGhee's prints on the broken bottleneck. It all ties in.'

Moss sucked the tip of his pencil then asked, 'Any luck at Fenn's house?'

'The break-in?' Elliot's good humour faded a little and he shook his head. 'Your gunman wore gloves. But we dug out the bullets that were fired and handed them over to the Professor.'

135

Clearing his throat mildly, MacMaster came in on cue. 'And as we anticipated, they match with the bullet which killed the – ah – Marquis. You have the gun you wanted, Thane.'

'Sam Hodge's gun,' said Thane thoughtfully.

'Hodge's?' echoed Elliot, looking round abruptly.

Thane nodded. 'Army Records confirm it. They called me at the hotel half an hour ago. Hodge was a despatch rider at Dunkirk – where he reported losing a .38 Webley during the evacuation. The serial numbers check.'

'Quite,' murmured MacMaster. His parchment face crinkled a little and he glanced at the watch on his wrist. 'I was in the Medical Corps myself. They – ah – issued excellent timepieces.'

Thane could have capped it with the story of the Kintyre contractor who'd souvenired a five-ton R.A.F. truck by building a haystack round it. But Elliot was muttering to himself, it would have been too easy to sidetrack.

'Hodge's gun, Fenn's house, Jennings' bull,' he para-phrased bleakly. 'All right, it doesn't make sense. Not yet. We put out a general alert for Hodge – and leak the fact at the afternoon press conference. I'll leave that with Elliot.'

The County detective nodded gloomily. Thane sat back, met MacMaster's mildly amused gaze, and drew a deep breath. 'You next, Professor.'

'Now?' MacMaster looked almost disappointed. He pre-ferred to come in late, enjoyed it. Particularly when the result was the ruination of all previous carefully con-structed theories. 'Well, if you insist.' He cleared his throat loudly 'I'll explain in suitable lay terminology.'

'Simple words for simple minds,' agreed Moss acidly.

'Exactly.' MacMaster inclined his head in complete, crushing concurrence. 'My official report will indicate that the post mortem examination was on a healthy adult male but – ah –' he broke off and glanced at Thane – 'I presume you're not really interested in casual detail like stomach contents?'

136

'They can wait,' said Thane gravely.

'Then we go straight to the fatal wound. Dissection of the tissues of the neck showed a punctured incised wound penetrating fractionally over four inches – with penetration of the internal jugular and pharynx.' He glanced at Moss. 'The pharynx is the musculo-membranous sac at the back of the mouth.'

'Over four inches?' queried Elliot sharply. 'That *skean dhu* blade is only about three inches long.'

MacMaster waved an indulgent hand. 'Correct. But a few practice stabbings in a University dissection room would illustrate the ease of disparity between the length of a peccant weapon and the depth of tissue penetrated. The blow – ah – shoves things in a bit, one might say. You have your murder weapon.' He stopped, took out a handkerchief, and blew his nose loudly. 'Of course, whether you have the person who used it is a very different matter.'

It took a few seconds for the full implication to sink home. Wordlessly, Thane shoved back his chair and walked over to the window. Outside, on the pavement, a photographer raised his camera. Thane shook his head and it was lowered again. He stared at his reflection in the glass for a moment then turned.

'We're listening, Professor.'

'Your reconstruction is of two men locked in combat.' MacMaster spoke with a calm, measured authority, as if he'd been on a lecture rostrum. 'Mine is based on interchange – cause has effect, effect has cause. I take the angle of penetration of this throat wound – an unusual angle. I take the mechanical ability of the human hand.' He rose, reached for Moss's pencil, took it, held it in his hand with the point uppermost, then stood behind him. 'Stay seated – and look down a little.'

Moss obeyed, puzzled.

The forensic expert moved his wrist till the pencil point was at the horizontal then his hand flicked in. The pencil stopped against Moss's throat.

'Like that?' said Thane softly.

'In my opinion, yes.' MacMaster nodded bleakly. 'MacGhee was probably seated at his desk when he was stabbed. And I can assure you once stabbed he would be in no condition to indulge in any brawl.' He tooth-sucked. 'Incidentally, I'm not completely happy about our finger-prints. Can anyone explain to me why they indicate the knife must have been held point down – for a blow struck in a slightly upward direction? Could we be – ah – dealing with two circus acrobats? Or is it possible MacGhee was standing on his head at the time?'

The cold sarcasm left them speechless.

'You –' Elliot swallowed hard and spoke first – 'you're saying Fenn didn't do it. But he was there. He was in the Land-Rover . . .'

'Exactly,' murmured MacMaster. 'The possibilities are intriguing.'

'Like what happened after Fenn was thumped with that bottle,' said Thane harshly. 'Elliot, let's go back on it. Was there anything odd, off-beat – no matter how small – from those fingerprint checks?'

It was easy to have hindsight now. Detective Inspector Elliot suddenly looked very wan and very tired. 'We couldn't get prints from the surgery and main door handles. They – well, they might have been wiped.'

'Then there's the knife itself,' mused Phil Moss. He gave a strangely sympathetic glance towards Elliot. 'If MacGhee often used it, shouldn't his prints have been there too?'

'They weren't.' The County detective put into words what the others were thinking. 'Suppose MacGhee knocked out Fenn with that bottle, then someone else arrived . . .'

'With everything ready for a perfect frame-up,' said Moss dryly. 'MacGhee as victim, Fenn as killer – and the Devil's Glen as a garbage disposal.'

'If we're right.' Thane chewed his lip for a moment.

'Professor, how'd you like to drive me over to Pitlochry hospital?'

'Delighted,' murmured MacMaster. 'Provided you give me a minute first – I always like to phone my stockbroker before noon.'

'I can wait.' Thane grimaced to himself, knowing a moment's jealousy. 'Elliot, you move out to Devil's Glen. There's a heavy recovery truck ordered from Perth – it should be starting work.'

Detective Inspector Elliot rose grimly to his feet and went out, MacMaster following.

Left alone in the room with him, Phil Moss gave a sudden dyspeptic chuckle. 'That old devil MacMaster . . . he loves it when he can pull something like this.' Then Moss sobered and used a long-nailed forefinger to scratch beneath his crumpled shirt collar. 'You played our own cards pretty close. Don't we bring Elliot in on the explosives side?'

'No. Because the top brass want that handled with care – the "care" spelled out in capital letters.' Thane shrugged. 'If Elliot knew – well, you or I might ask a wrong question and get away with it. If Elliot asked the same question people might remember he was on the original inquiry. We keep it to ourselves – no one else involved.'

Which wasn't strictly accurate, he knew. A growing number of men in several places had begun to scurry around.

A long telephone call to Buddha Ilford had started things moving that morning. The Glasgow C.I.D. chief had initially staged a minor explosion of his own, his scepticism undisguised, his suggestion that the Braedale air had gone to Thane's head. But Special Branch had come into the act. And Special Branch, already in a state of nervous twitter about the coming Children of the Mist rally, were against taking chances. Every member of Jennings' Glasgow committee would go under immediate surveillance. A

139

short leet of possible targets was being put under discreet emergency guard.

And Colin Thane had been left with the distinct impression that for his sake something somewhere had better be found all ready to go bang.

On the other hand, Phil Moss's share had been a typical digging job . . . a long-shot inspiration which had paid off handsomely.

He'd located the Glasgow hire firm which had rented out the van used in the Dunkeld armoury raid. Taken for a straight 24-hour period, the vehicle's records showed it had clocked up 232 miles' travel before it was found abandoned on the fringe of the city.

Glasgow to Dunkeld and back was a round trip of under 160 miles. The difference was exactly what would have been required to allow a detour through Braedale on the return trip.

And photographs of the Glasgow committee, prised out of Special Branch's political files – something they didn't like even admitting existed – were now on their way round to the van hire office.

'Life gets complicated,' pronounced Moss. He shook his head at Thane's offer of a cigarette. 'I'm giving them up. Margaret Linton's got some pretty strong views on nicotine acid and stomach ulcers – and that port wine idea she gave me certainly works.' He slapped his scrawny stomach. 'This hasn't even said hello all morning. Eh . . . what do you hope to get over at the hospital?'

'MacMaster's opinion on Fenn plus the chance of another talk with mother and daughter.' Thane lit a cigarette of his own and blew the smoke ruthlessly in his friend's direction. 'Time is running out for us on the explosives deal. But even if you set that aside – well, if Charlie Fenn's in the clear, who do we go for on the murder?'

Moss grunted. 'Hodge?'

'That's what most people would call the logical answer.' Thane glanced at his watch. 'Well, at least you're going to get your glass of port – I want you to take Margaret Linton to lunch. In fact, I invited her on your behalf. She'll be here at twelve.'

'Eh?' Moss shot upright. 'Now look . . .'

'For a reason,' soothed Thane. 'Phil, get her to pay a professional visit to Broomvale Farm this afternoon – she can make brave noises that the animals come before any kind of mourning. You'll follow her there on the excuse you had to contact her with some inquiry detail. Then take a wander around.'

'Why?' Moss glared suspiciously.

Thane sighed. 'All right, I'll spell it out. I want to know how Dougan and Jennings react to the fact that we want Sam Hodge.'

'Do I tell them he shot the Marquis?'

'His gun shot the Marquis,' corrected Thane in a gentle voice. 'Phil, that blasted bull could be the key to a lot of things.' He stubbed his half-smoked cigarette, headed for the door, then stopped and twisted a wry, lop-sided grin. 'But I don't think Hodge pulled the trigger. I think Hodge is dead.'

Phil Moss found himself spluttering to an empty room.

Chapter Seven

Travel aboard Professor MacMaster's massive old Daimler was neither fast nor particularly comfortable. It was early afternoon when the wine-coloured limousine trundled out of the wooded hills and reached Pitlochry.

They hadn't eaten, which didn't particularly worry Thane. But the tall, bony forensic expert stopped at the first hotel, unfolded himself from behind the wheel, and insisted that lunch was an immediate priority.

Thane decided not to argue. They ate beside a window overlooking the broad, placid sweep of Loch Faskally and the winding, leisurely River Tummel, the romantic song-and-story starting place of the Road to the Isles. But in the middle distance the grey concrete bulk of the giant Tummel-Garry hydro-electric dam was a reminder times had changed.

'Excellently cooked – and a change of diet does wonders for the intestinal tract.' MacMaster happily forked another morsel of pink, firm-fleshed salmon into his mouth, chewed with a denture-clacking precision, then gestured across the water. 'Thoughtful people, those hydro-electric fellows. I was shown over the dam and generating station once. They've a salmon ladder to let fish climb the dam and get upstream to spawn.'

Thane nodded absently, only half-listening as MacMaster went on. The version he'd heard was that the fish-ladder had been a low-cost addition to soothe some of the inevitable howls about scenic desecration when the project was first mooted. Not that the diehards could have blocked the plan. A complex of nine power stations with a multimega-watt capacity was the size of argument which overcame most opposition, created too major a national asset.

He jerked a little at the thought. If Adam Jennings was looking around for something sensational to blow up . . .

'Am I by any faint chance boring you?' demanded Mac-Master suddenly.

'Sorry.' Thane forced an apologetic grin and pushed the possibility aside for the moment. 'I've got a lot on my mind, Professor.'

'Including Fenn's possible concussion?' MacMaster's fork and knife carefully dissected another piece of salmon and he chewed for a moment. 'That should be simple to establish. He doesn't remember being actually struck on the head?'

'No. There's a blank till he woke up with the Land-Rover on top of him.'

'Retrograde amnesia.' MacMaster nodded happily. 'Your true amnesia – usually restricted to a matter of seconds or minutes before injury. There's the occasional genuine retro-grade case going back for a few days, of course. But anything longer is at best a text-book freak or rooted in hysteria.' He pushed his plate aside and rubbed his hands. 'Now – coffee?'

Thane gave up. When they were ready to leave Mac-Master insisted on paying the bill then equally insisted on obtaining a receipt for his expense sheet.

They walked the short distance to the district hospital, a modest-sized building in grey stone. Once inside the doors the elderly forensic expert took one sniff of the antiseptic-laced air, sighed happily, then beckoned a passing nurse. Within moments the result was a dutiful convoy of two doctors and a slightly flustered matron.

'Patient first,' decided MacMaster. 'Then I want all avail-able X-ray plates.'

143

The convoy murmured agreement.

Inspector Fenn was in a side-room at the entrance to one of the wards. Told to wait, Thane watched the small procession troop in then grinned as a uniformed police sergeant came out frowning. The door closed with an emphatic click.

'Thrown out, sergeant?'

'Aye.' The man straightened his shoulders at the sight of Thane's warrant card. 'Well, at least it gets me off my backside for a spell – I've been sitting beside that bed most o' the day.'

'How is he?' asked Thane.

The sergeant shrugged. 'They haven't told me anything, sir. Who's the old fellow that went in with them?'

'MacMaster.' The name registered and Thane smiled a little. 'Got anything out of Inspector Fenn so far?'

The man shook his head. 'Mostly he's been asleep. His wife and the girl got in for a spell this morning, but he didn't talk much.'

'They're still here?'

The sergeant nodded. 'Aye, in one of the doctors' rooms. Mrs Fenn seems pleasant enough, but her daughter looks pretty timid.'

'That's recent,' said Thane grimly.

They stood there while long minutes ticked past on a wall clock. Then, at last, the door swung open again and the convoy trooped out, the matron carrying a small bowl covered by a cloth.

'Tag along, Thane,' invited MacMaster briskly. 'You might find this moderately interesting.'

Thane left the sergeant and followed. They went to a small pathology laboratory where MacMaster took the bowl and sent the matron on her way with a murmured compliment. Whatever he said, it made her blush pink and retire with something close to a giggle.

'The rest of you will remain quiet and keep that damned door closed,' said MacMaster in a crisp, business-like com-

144

mand. He glanced at Thane and the two doctors. 'Anyone wishing to cough, blow his nose or cause any similar disturbance will do so now – not later.' He gave them a moment, nodded, and turned to the laboratory bench.

Occasionally humming under his breath, the tall, angular figure worked with an unhurried precision. Wondering what was going on, Thane raised an eyebrow at the nearest of the medical men, drew a swift, negative head-shake, and leaned back against the wall with a sigh.

MacMaster crossed to a microscope, fiddled with it for a moment, then hunched over the eyepiece. A faint smile on his gaunt face, he at last turned and beckoned the doctor beside Thane.

'You, young Harris – take a look. If you paid suitable attention to my lectures in your ill-spent student days it may help you understand.'

'Young Harris', bald and middle-aged, did as he was told.

'It's – ah – an excellent specimen, sir,' he said cautiously.

'Which means you don't know what the hell you're supposed to look for,' said MacMaster icily. He sniffed and switched his attention. 'Thane, so far the clinical picture comes down to a severe blow having been sustained. X-rays show a hairline fracture of the skull, the scalp has a pattern of small, incised wounds and there's considerable bruising and contusion. All caused, in my professional opinion, by a single blow – one which would render him unconscious for some time. I think my colleagues will agree he would certainly qualify as a possible retrograde amnesia.'

The two white coats made quick mumbling noises and MacMaster acknowledged with a nod.

'However . . .' He held up an attention-demanding forefinger. 'We still have to establish whether injury could have been sustained at MacGhee's surgery or when the Land-Rover crashed. Correct?'

'It's what we need,' admitted Thane reluctantly. 'But can we do it?'

'In this instance, quite easily.' MacMaster gestured towards the microscope. 'Your proof is a sample of hair collected from the vicinity of Fenn's scalp wounds. Thane, hit a man on the head with a blunt instrument and you can split the surface tissue. But –' the forefinger wagged again – 'under microscopic examination the hair fibres and roots will only show evidence of crushing. Hit the same man with a sharp instrument and the fibres and roots are quite clearly cut. Fenn's samples show both crushing and cutting took place. Which means the bottle MacGhee used as a weapon – a blunt instrument which shattered and cut on impact.'

'Nice going,' admitted Thane softly. Then he frowned. 'But Fenn was bounced around when that Land-Rover crashed. Couldn't . . .'

'Couldn't something similar have happened then?' Mac-Master gave a small, quiet smile of satisfaction. 'I'm always sure before I state an opinion, Thane. And I happened to find a few particles of unmistakable bottle glass around the wound. That should – ah – satisfy the most stubborn unbeliever.'

Thane drew a deep breath. He should have known MacMaster's technique of keeping the most simple, most practical point of all till last.

MacMaster still hadn't finished. 'Conclusions, Thane. Charles Fenn couldn't have stabbed MacGhee after sustaining that blow on the head. MacGhee certainly couldn't have dealt the blow after being stabbed. And similarly, Fenn would be unconscious for some time after the blow – which means he couldn't have driven the Land-Rover. There's a further test remaining, of course, but it will take time. Fenn's clothes were bloodstained when he arrived here. We'll check the blood for grouping – Fenn is Group O, MacGhee was Group A. But even if both are present your Inspector Fenn can be guilty of nothing worse than taking part in a common brawl.'

'I'd like to tell him,' said Thane quietly.

'Go ahead,' invited MacMaster. 'Just remember he's still under a certain amount of sedation.'

Thane left them, went along to the side-room, and found the sergeant smoking a cigarette outside. He gestured him to stay where he was and went in. The hospital bed was immediately under a window, only Fenn's bandaged head visible above the smooth white sheets. Fenn's face was pale but his eyes were open – and their tired gaze suddenly widened.

'Thane!' It came as a hoarse, forced whisper.

'Relax,' said Thane cheerfully. He found a chair, brought it over, and sat down. 'This is mostly a social call. How's the leg? I thought you'd be strung up in one of those traction-pulley affairs.'

'Later. They – they're having another go at me this afternoon.' Fenn licked his lips, an effort in itself. 'I heard you got me out. Thanks.'

'Sergeant Imrie's lifting jack did most of it,' Thane told him mildly.

The bandaged head shook slightly. 'I heard different. And – well, I heard about MacGhee. Nurses talking.' His eyes were bright and very anxious. 'Thane, what's the score?'

'As far as you're concerned?' Thane considered him soberly for a moment. 'Charlie, I'd say you've been damned lucky. But you're in the clear now.'

'Now?' Fenn was too much of a cop to let the obvious slip by. 'Meaning I was all lined up for it earlier.' He gave a slow sigh of relief. 'And not much I could have done about it. Whatever happened, there's a complete blank. I was tussling with MacGhee and – well, then the film breaks.'

'You were thumped on the head.' Thane sat back. 'After that, all the signs are someone did a pretty fair job of trying

147

to frame you. And you made things easy enough for them by the way you've been acting.'

Fenn frowned and croaked a protest. 'I – I'd reasons.'

'Including Sylvia's car crash escapade.' Thane saw the question forming and shook his head. 'No, I haven't spread that around. There's no need.'

'Good.' Fenn closed his eyes for a moment then asked, 'Who tried to frame me? Could it –' his mouth twisted wryly – 'well, I've still got to ask the obvious. Could it be Jennings?'

'He's got a moderately good alibi,' mused Thane. 'So far, we've been too busy concentrating on you. But I'll tell you this for free, if you keep it quiet – your hunch about Jennings and the armoury raid is shaping into something positive.'

'You mean it?' Charles Fenn stared at him with an open relief. 'Then maybe I haven't been going completely crazy. I've had time to wonder about that.'

'So had the rest of us,' said Thane dryly. He shoved back the chair and rose. 'I'd better leave before I'm thrown out. But we'll let you know how things shape.'

The man wriggled up a fraction, wincing. 'Mind doing me a favour?'

'Within reason,' answered Thane cautiously.

'My wife and young Sylvia. Tell them that it looks like everything's all right.' Fenn gnawed his lip. 'I didn't say much to them earlier. I was – hell, I was too busy wondering if maybe I had . . .' He didn't finish.

'I'll tell them,' promised Thane. 'Now do everybody a good turn. Stay out of trouble.'

Fenn managed a grin then sank back against the pillow, his eyes closing again.

Thane went out quietly, told the County sergeant the watch could end, then had the man guide him along to where Fenn's wife and daughter were waiting. It was a small room, at the end of a corridor which ran through the

148

hospital's office area. The door was half-open and he knocked lightly as he went in.

'I wondered when you'd come, Mr Thane,' said Isobel Fenn in a tight resolute voice. She was alone in the room, sitting in a chair, her eyes heavily shadowed from lack of sleep, a woman both tired and desperately worried. 'You – you've seen Charlie?'

'I've just left him.' He saw her hands tighten on her lap and smiled a quick reassurance, feeling it a change to bring good news to someone for once. 'He says everything looks like being all right now. And I'd say the same. Your husband may be a stubborn devil, Mrs Fenn. But he hasn't killed anyone.'

She simply stared at him at first, apparently ready to either laugh or cry – maybe both. Then she drew a deep breath and, fingers trembling, opened her handbag and brought out a lipstick and a comb.

'I'll go and see him.'

'He'd like that,' Thane told her. 'Where's Sylvia?'

'Outside. I told her she needed some fresh air.' Isobel Fenn gestured towards the window and began a quick job of tidying her hair.

Thane went over, looked out, and raised an eyebrow. Long hair caught back by a clasp, wearing slacks and a jersey, Sylvia Fenn was standing in a small patch of garden beside a tiny ornamental pond. She wasn't alone. By her side and talking earnestly was Dave Anderson. The young red-headed ex-student said something more then, as she nodded, he took her hand in an oddly protective gesture.

'How long has he been here?' asked Thane mildly.

'Dave?' Finished combing her hair, Isobel Fenn used the lipstick quickly then gave a fractional smile. 'He came over this morning to see if he could help. Then he decided to stay.'

'Because of Sylvia?'

'I've got my own man, Mr Thane.' She said it softly and

149

returned the lipstick to her handbag. 'Dave's been around before. And he knows all that happened. I think – well, this time Sylvia's grown up a little, learned a few things the hard way.'

'Plenty of people do,' said Thane. He scratched his head. 'Well, I was going to offer you a lift back to Braedale. But . . .'

'Dave's got a car.' She nodded, sharing his understanding. 'We'll let him take care of things.' Rising, she started for the door then looked back. 'Mr Thane, will Charlie be fit enough to keep on in the force?'

Thane shrugged. 'I wouldn't like to guess. That leg . . .'

'It won't bother me if he can't,' she said quietly. 'It won't bother me at all.'

She went out. After a moment Thane went back to the window. Her daughter and Dave Anderson were still standing beside the ornamental pond, still holding hands.

He grinned to himself, turned away, and decided to find MacMaster.

Detective Inspector Phil Moss drove his borrowed County force Mini up to the grey stone walls of Broomvale Farm, parked the vehicle neatly behind Margaret Linton's empty fastback Sunbeam Stiletto, and glanced at his watch. It was 3 p.m., the time they'd agreed.

Not that there'd been a particularly enthusiastic reception for the idea when he'd broached it over lunch. Margaret Linton had made some sharp-edged noises about professional conduct before she'd finally agreed. But she'd come. And the next stage was up to him.

He left the car, strolled round under the shadow of the ancient castle walls, and reached the cattle pens. A minor rodeo seemed in progress at one of the lower pens and he headed towards it – then stopped, gaping.

Inside the enclosure was a large, angry-looking black Angus bull. Approaching the animal, making gentle croon-

150

ing noises as she went, Margaret Linton walked slowly with her right hand hidden behind her back. Two grinning farmhands, one with a rope, stood just outside the pen's stout fencework.

Moss swallowed hard and came nearer.

Still crooning, Margaret Linton reached the bull. Her left hand began to stroke its neck and the animal snorted. But it didn't move away and she stroked on, working along its back, taking her time. Then, as she reached its hindquarters, her right hand suddenly swung forward. For a fraction of a second sunlight glinted on the bright steel of a heavy-gauge hypodermic needle . . . before it buried deep in the bull's flesh.

As she sprang clear, half a ton of irate, pained Aberdeen Angus erupted in anger. Head tossing, bellowing, the bull lumbered round with surprising speed to settle with its surprise enemy. But Margaret Linton was already on the safe side of the fence. She looked over, saw Moss, waved, then signalled to the farmhands. They entered the pen cautiously, the man with the rope widening the loop at one end.

'Come to see the show, Inspector?' The slow, cynical drawl made him turn. Boots mud-spattered, Tommy Dougan stood a few paces behind him. The head cattleman's broken-toothed grin was far from friendly. 'Maybe the boss should charge admission.'

Moss grunted, eyeing the man with calculated indifference. 'Business, Dougan. I want to talk to Miss Linton.'

'After she's finished earnin' her fee.' Dougan spat casually on the concrete near his feet. 'What's it about? How Charlie Fenn croaked MacGhee?'

Moss shrugged, watching the pen again. Their first attempt with the rope a failure, the two farmhands circled the snorting bull again. The hypodermic needle still quivered in its rear.

'We don't think Fenn's our man,' he said suddenly turn-

151

ing. 'It could be an old pal of yours, Sam Hodge. We're looking for him.'

'Hodge?' Dougan controlled his surprise well then frowned, the white line of the scar above his left eye twisting. 'That's a pretty crazy idea.' Then he snickered. 'Better than havin' to charge a cop with murder, I suppose.'

'Maybe.' Moss answered stiffly but refused to be drawn. 'Where's Adam Jennings?'

'Out,' answered Dougan shortly. 'Why?'

Moss sighed. 'Sonny, you ask too many questions. Too many by far. I thought I'd tell him about the Hodge development.'

'Makes no odds to us.' Dougan scraped a hand over his unshaven chin. 'Old Sam wasn't pullin' his weight. So he was sacked an' left – weeks ago.'

Moss nodded indifferently. The farmhands were ready again, the rope swung, and this time its noose went round the Angus bull's thick, muscular neck. The two men scampered to anchor the other end of the rope round a fence post, the noose tightened, and the animal came to a sudden, puzzled halt, shaking its head.

Margaret Linton slipped into the enclosure from the rear, the brass barrel of a veterinary syringe in her hand. She reached the glinting steel needle, screwed the barrel home with two quick half-turns, and triggered the plunger. Before the bull realized anything had happened she had the needle out and was back outside the fencing. The farmhands slacked off the rope and the animal, bewildered, prowled around in a snorting, defensive circle.

'She's finished,' said Dougan curtly. 'I'll tell the boss you were around – when I see him.'

He went off, heading towards another of the pens. Moss stuck his hands in his pockets and wandered over to Margaret Linton. She was packing her equipment away and he winced as he saw the steel needle in close-up.

'Sometimes I feel pretty sorry for animals,' he mused.

She laughed, brushed a lock of greying hair back from her forehead, then snapped the veterinary bag shut. 'It was a plain, ordinary antibiotic shot – I said he looked a bit watery-eyed and that I'd better give him it.' She glanced around to make sure no one was near then added, 'Well, I couldn't just hang about waiting for you. It won't do him any particular good, but it certainly won't harm him. What about you?'

'I talked to Dougan,' Moss told her. 'But that's it – he says Adam Jennings isn't here.'

She frowned. 'Then he's lying, Phil. I'm certain I saw Jennings as I arrived. In the distance, I'll admit. But it was him.'

'Where?'

'Down beyond the pens.' She gestured with her head. 'Near that old dovecote. I think he went into it.'

Moss looked. The dovecote, a small round tower about twelve feet high and topped by a conical roof, was about three hundred yards away. It looked old enough to have been part of the original castle out-buildings. But now, with weeds growing from the crumbling stone walls and the roof patched with rusted corrugated iron, it was a derelict ruin.

'We could wander down,' he said hopefully. 'Got a minute?'

She sighed but nodded and picked up her bag. They'd passed the cattle pens and were on their way across the final stretch of open ground towards the tower when there was a shout then hurrying footsteps. Stopping, they turned and waited until a panting, swearing Tommy Dougan caught up with them.

'Where the hell are you goin'?' demanded Dougan with a breathless lack of ceremony.

'Just looking around,' said Moss calmly. 'I wanted to take a look inside the tower.'

'Then I should damned well let you, mister.' Dougan's mouth twisted angrily. 'Except we've lost one vet already

153

– an' we need Miss Linton. That ruddy place is ready to fall down if anyone breathes too hard on it. Nobody goes in – boss's orders.'

'Like that?' Moss shrugged, took a few steps nearer, looked at the dovecote again, then came back. 'Better do what he says, Margaret.' He gave Dougan a wintry glance. 'I wouldn't like to put anyone to the trouble of digging us out.'

Dougan grunted and stayed where he was while they turned and walked back towards the cars. Phil Moss didn't glance back. He didn't need to any more.

There was a bare patch of earth just outside the dovecote door. A bare patch with a less than half-smoked cigarette lying to one side, partly flattened into the earth by a large sized shoe-print.

If Adam Jennings had been inside, why had he been so shy about showing himself – and why so careful about getting rid of his cigarette before he entered?

It might be interesting to find out.

Colin Thane and Professor MacMaster were last back at Braedale police station. It was late afternoon when the Daimler rolled to a majestic halt in the police yard, but they walked into the building to an unusually cheerful greeting.

'What's going on?' Thane looked around the group of grinning faces in the outer office.

Margaret Linton answered, glancing wryly at Moss. 'I've had to stand here and listen to a highly slanderous account of what Phil calls the Broomvale Circus.'

'Call it assault with a deadly weapon on a perfectly innocent animal,' said Moss dead-pan. In the background, Sergeant Imrie and Detective Inspector Elliot chuckled agreement.

'Sir.' Imrie stepped forward, his manner becoming more serious. 'Thanks for phoning through about Inspector Fenn. The lads appreciated it.'

154

Thane nodded mildly. He'd made a few telephone calls before he'd left Pitlochry, including one to Special Branch which had added the Tummel Dam to the potential target list. But he had something else on his mind. It had seemed strangely quiet outside. The press team had vanished and there had been no sign of the Children of the Mist on the opposite side of the road.

Elliot answered his query. 'Ach, the press boys are happy with the story that we're trying to find Sam Hodge.' He grimaced. 'Not that we've had any luck, just a few false alarm reports that he'd been sighted.'

'All we can do is keep working on it,' said Thane neutrally. But his feelings hadn't changed. If Sam Hodge did turn up alive that, for him, would be the real surprise. 'And the Children?'

'I don't know what happened there,' admitted Elliot. 'Maybe they got tired hanging about in the cold. They just packed it in and left – that would be about an hour ago.'

Thane nodded. The timing was right if Dave Anderson had made a telephone call from the hospital and broken the news about Fenn. He'd need to have another talk with that young redhead, and soon.

'Ah – Thane . . .' Professor MacMaster eased forward, glancing significantly at Margaret Linton.

He introduced them. The pathologist's tight, parchment face crinkled into something approaching pleasure.

'I've always had a particular sympathy for the veterinary profession, Miss Linton,' he murmured. 'It's rather like my own branch of medicine. On the average, cases that come my way are – ah – no longer able to tell anyone about their complaint. I've got to look for the causes unaided.'

'That bull out at Broomvale was complaining loud enough,' said Moss. 'And I didn't blame it. If anyone tried to stick that size of needle in my backside –' he gave a mock shudder at the prospect – 'well, I'd just keep running.'

'If you're talking about the Earl . . .' began Margaret Linton.

'The Earl?' queried Thane.

'That's his name,' she explained. 'Earl of Broomvale – one of the best bulls left in Adam Jennings' herd. He has always been pretty temperamental, like plenty of males.' She sighed a little. 'The Marquis was different – a sweetie to work with. I didn't see him much, but you could do almost anything to that bull and he wouldn't complain.'

Elliot opened his mouth to say something but changed his mind and let Thane speak first.

'You got the Land-Rover out of that river?'

'Eventually,' agreed the County man. 'They've taken it back to Perth, and the Scientific boys will give it a look over. Charlie Fenn's .22 rifle was in the back, but I didn't find anything else that seemed to matter.'

MacMaster fidgeted a little and glanced at his wrist-watch. 'Thane, I'd like to make a phone call. My stock-broker . . .'

'You've earned it,' said Thane easily. 'Sergeant . . .'

As Imrie led MacMaster off to a telephone, Thane quietly signalled to Moss and they eased out too, leaving Elliot talking to Margaret Linton. Thane noticed the strangely earnest expression on the County man's face, but let it pass.

They went into Inspector Fenn's office. Thane glanced at the telephone message pad on the desk, saw Buddha Ilford had called twice from Glasgow, then looked up.

'What happened at Broomvale, Phil?'

Moss told him and he whistled.

'Suppose Jennings wanted somewhere safe to hide that load of demolition charges but didn't want to have the stuff sitting under him in the farmhouse . . .'

'Where it might go off bang?' Moss nodded cynical agreement. 'That way he might have a nasty accident.'

156

'And get more than a draught up his kilt,' said Thane grimly. 'All right, we'll go take a look at this dovecote.'

'When?'

Thane chewed his lip for a moment. 'Not while anyone's likely to be around, Phil. We'll leave it till late. And Dougan played the innocent about Sam Hodge?'

'Uh-huh.' Moss sniffed hard. 'What makes you sure things are different in that direction?'

'The whole pattern,' declared Thane slumping down in a chair. 'Hodge vanishes immediately he is fired. Nobody sees him – not even when he collects his stuff from that cottage. Suppose stage one is that something happens to Hodge. Then stage two could be that someone – anyone, because the place isn't locked – collects his things when the cottage is empty.'

'And the .38 is in his trunk,' mused Moss. 'Colin, there happens to be a hell of a lot after that which doesn't make any kind of sense. If you're saying that either Jennings or Dougan did for Hodge and got that gun then . . .'

'I know,' nodded Thane ruefully. 'Back to the Marquis. Why shoot that damned bull? I double-checked the records – both MacGhee's file and Margaret Linton's. It was in perfect health. Which made it a hell of an expensive killing if it was just to frame Fenn . . .'

'And if the long-term idea was to murder John MacGhee – I give up.' Moss bit his lip briefly. The truce with his ulcer seemed to have ended, that old familiar ache was building. 'My advice is not to decide you've got to be right. That's how Fenn came unstuck.' He gave a lop-sided grin at Thane's crude, one-word answer. 'All right, correction. Fenn's hunch about the armoury raid paid off. You still haven't told Elliot?'

'Soon,' promised Thane. The telephone beside him rang as he spoke. He gave Moss a shrug and answered.

'And about time,' grated Buddha Ilford's voice over the wire. 'Where the devil have you been, Thane? Off on a scenic tour of the Highlands?'

157

'I'm just in, sir. Old MacMaster doesn't believe in fast driving.' Thane grimaced across at Moss. 'I tried to contact you from Pitlochry . . .'

'I got the message when I came in,' rasped Ilford. 'But for half the damned day I've been out arguing the toss with a couple of Her Majesty's tax inspectors.'

'As long as you ended up winning . . .' Thane stopped as a bear-like growl reached his ears.

'Winning? How can anyone win against those bloodsuckers?' demanded Ilford. 'They've damned nearly taken the shirt off my back. Let's talk about Fenn. You're positive he's in the clear over the MacGhee killing?'

'Completely.'

'Then at least someone's happy,' said Ilford, somewhat mollified. 'And it makes life for the rest of us a little easier when we're not putting a cop into the dock. The Scientific Branch report backs you up on the bull affair, if you're still interested. There was no trace of blood or bovidae hairs on Fenn's car or on the clothes you sent down – Fenn hadn't been romping around any bull-rings. But you can tell him they noticed he'd a slight touch of dandruff.'

'I don't think that will worry him too much,' murmured Thane.

Ilford barked a laugh. 'I've another reason for calling. We're beginning to get places with those Children of the Mist. There's an identification from the self-drive outfit which hired out the van used in the armoury raid.'

Thane breathed a silent thanks to whoever had accomplished the legwork involved, found his cigarettes, and lit one as Ilford talked on.

'Their booking office clerk identified one of the photographs we prised out of Special Branch. The van was rented by a member of the Glasgow committee, Hamilton Campbell.'

'Middle-aged with a beard,' said Thane briefly. 'Right now he's a one-third share of Adam Jennings' alibi for the time when John MacGhee was stabbed.'

'He could be important in another way,' said Ilford crisply. 'Campbell is in the publishing game. But he has a brother who works for a construction firm. It's a long shot – but that firm has sub-contracted on plenty of major projects. One was your Tummel Dam. Another is that new multi-storey office extension to St Andrew's House in Edinburgh. Top-level Government administration accommodation, Thane. And only opened last month – how's that for a target?'

Thane said nothing, the idea was so simple and so exactly tailored. St Andrew's House was administration centre for Scotland. Or, from the Nationalist viewpoint, a local branch office for English government.

'Like to bet on it?' queried Ilford dryly. 'Your dam against my office-block? It looks like we'll have to have a long talk with Campbell.'

Which was the last thing Thane wanted. 'That might not help,' he warned quickly. 'Even if we nailed him on some kind of charge the others could simply change the plan – go for something else now or later. And there's the situation up here, sir. Suppose I say I might end up bringing two charges of murder against Jennings . . .'

'Two?' queried Ilford sharply.

'Sam Hodge.' Thane ignored Phil Moss's shudder of warning. 'Couldn't Campbell wait till morning? I need more time.'

'I've heard that one before,' said Ilford reluctantly. He sighed. 'All right. But the Lord help us all if anything goes up with a bang overnight. Anything else?'

'No,' said Thane. 'Except – well, I heard there'd been a minor misunderstanding at Millside Division. Detective Constable Beech . . .'

'Beech?' Ilford made it sound like an obscenity. 'Not now, Thane. I'll talk about it later – once you've got this bunch of hairy-kneed fanatics out of what's left of my hair.'

159

The faraway receiver slammed down. Sadly, Thane replaced his own.

'Bad timing,' said Moss with minimal sympathy. He yawned then mid-way through it became a belch. 'What now?'

'You hold the fort,' decided Thane, rising. 'I'm going to have that talk with Elliot, then see if Dave Anderson is back.'

Going out, he found Sergeant Imrie on duty at the inquiry desk but the place otherwise deserted.

'Seen D.I. Elliot?' asked Thane.

'He's out, sir.' Imrie looked mildly perplexed. 'Left about five minutes ago with Professor MacMaster and Miss Linton. They didn't say where they were going.'

Puzzled, Thane turned towards the door. Then he came to a sudden halt, wondering what was due to happen next. Adam Jennings had just entered from the street.

'The man I want – good.' Jennings came straight towards him. But a changed Jennings from their last encounter. This was a return of the easy-going, benevolently mild giant – with a black mourning tie knotted neatly at his shirt collar. His voice was muted and suitably friendly. 'Chief Inspector, I heard Moss visited the farm looking for me. I thought I'd better come over.'

Thane nodded coolly. 'It wasn't important.'

'Well, I wasn't far away – just out in the fields.' Jennings spread his large hands apologetically. 'Tommy Dougan isn't particularly co-operative with visitors, I'm afraid.' He came closer. 'Dougan said you're suddenly interested in old Sam Hodge. And I've heard a whisper that we might have been wrong about Inspector Fenn.'

'We?' Thane raised a sardonic eyebrow.

'That maybe I was, then,' surrendered Jennings.

Thane shrugged. 'All I can say is we want to talk to Hodge. Charlie Fenn isn't under any kind of arrest – and won't be.'

'I see.' Jennings rubbed a hand across his forehead. 'It

160

doesn't leave me with a very pleasant character reference. But John MacGhee was a good friend – and everything seemed to point the one way, towards Fenn.'

'It doesn't now,' said Thane heavily. 'Is that why you withdrew the Children picket-line?'

'The vigil?' Jennings stopped short then cleared his throat hastily and forced a smile. 'Yes. Things began to appear uncertain and it didn't seem such a good idea.'

For Thane, the moment of covered-up confusion had been enough. Jennings hadn't called off the youngsters, hadn't realized they were gone, couldn't have been contacted by Dave Anderson. Which might – very well could – matter a lot.

'Well, you know we're looking for Sam Hodge,' he said easily. 'Any idea where he might have headed after he left you?'

Jennings shook his head. 'Things weren't exactly friendly when he went. But I know he had friends or a relative of some kind in Glasgow.'

'A sister – he hasn't contacted her.'

'Sam Hodge.' Jennings shoved his hands deep in his jacket pockets. 'I just can't figure him as . . .' He stopped and shrugged. 'You're the detective, Thane. I've learned my lesson. But just in case you need me for anything more, I'd better tell you now – I'm leaving for Glasgow early tomorrow and I won't be back before Monday.'

'Still going ahead with the rally.' Thane made it more statement than question.

Jennings nodded. 'Sunday, as arranged. But we'll need tomorrow for some of the final preparations.' He paused and smiled a little. 'There is a small matter I'd like to tidy first, though. Well, not so small – the Marquis's carcase is still lying in Allison's chill room. Can we get rid of it – say tomorrow sometime?'

On the surface it was a reasonable enough request. Thane hesitated then agreed.

'Good,' said Jennings, satisfied. 'I know Allison has his

own ideas about using the meat. But he's not on. The Public Health squad would have a fit. And anyway, I'm damned if I'd allow it. The Marquis was special – I'd rather see him decently cremated. I'll get Dougan to take care of the details.'

'He's welcome,' said Thane wryly. 'Got your speech written for Sunday?'

'It's written all right,' said Jennings. He considered Thane strangely for a moment then gave a soft chuckle. 'Don't worry, Chief Inspector. You'll hear all about it. I've a feeling most people will.'

He gave a brief nod of farewell and left the station. Thane went to the door, watched him climb into a large blue Rover coupe, and waited until the car had driven off.

The light was beginning to fade a little. In another hour it would be dusk. A few more, and it would be his turn to visit Jennings – though in a very different fashion.

He lit a cigarette, stuffed the pack back in his pocket, and began walking towards the village filling station and Dave Anderson.

The same man was on duty at the garage pumps. He greeted Thane with a wave and, without being asked, thumbed towards the back.

Thane went round to the wooden hut at the rear of the building. As he reached it, he could hear a muffled, indistinct murmur of voices. That stopped when he knocked on the door. A moment passed, then Dave Anderson opened it and looked out.

'Hello, Dave.' Thane gave him a friendly nod. 'Can I come in?'

Anderson frowned slightly, looked over his shoulder, then nodded. 'Squeeze through,' he invited. 'I've got company already.'

There were three other young men inside. They eyed Thane warily, nodded at Anderson's introduction. Then,

162

the oldest, who looked still short of twenty-one, reached for an anorak lying on the workbench beside him.

'We were getting ready to leave anyway,' he said in brief explanation. 'All right, Dave?'

'We can finish it tomorrow,' agreed Anderson.

The trio trooped out. Anderson heeled the door shut again, saw Thane looking at the strange collection of wires and coils lying on the workbench, and grinned.

'Just a gadget we're trying to dream up, Chief Inspector.'

'It certainly didn't ever come out of a TV set,' mused Thane. 'What is it? Some kind of electro-magnet?' Which was more than an inspired guess. Kate's junior science class had used one in a project last term. He'd spent an entire evening trying to help her get some right answers to the homework questions which followed – and had failed.

'You're halfway right,' agreed Anderson, slightly surprised. 'We thought we'd try and build a magnetic field test rig.' He showed amusement at Thane's blank reception. 'For metal testing – things like engine crankshafts, con rods, smaller parts. Put a part in the rig, pass a current, and you'll get a reading that'll detect any hidden flaws. This one's only a toy.'

'I'll take your word for it.' Thane leaned against the bench. 'I saw you over at Pitlochry, Dave. Did they come back with you?'

'Sylvia and her mother?' Anderson nodded. 'Looks like there's going to be a long queue of people lining up to apologize to Charlie Fenn.'

'Including you?'

'More or less.' The young redhead grimaced. 'We all make mistakes.'

'That's what Adam Jennings said about ten minutes ago.' Thane watched his face, but there was a complete lack of reaction. 'You knew about Sylvia and that car crash, knew it all along, didn't you?'

163

Anderson nodded slightly. 'The next morning, anyway. She – well, she wanted a shoulder to cry on and mine is fairly waterproof.' He picked up a small screwdriver and used the tip of the blade to remove a speck of dirt from under one fingernail. 'Are you really looking for Sam Hodge? Or is it just a convenient smokescreen for – well, something else.'

'Suppose you tell me,' countered Thane.

'I wouldn't know.' The supple fingers twirled the screwdriver round then suddenly stabbed the blade into the wood of the bench. 'Think you'll get him – whoever he was?'

'That's what I'm paid for, Dave.' Thane kept his approach unhurriedly casual. 'Thanks for lifting that protest vigil from the station – it made the place look untidy.'

The redhead looked at him, grinned a little, and said nothing.

'Jennings leaves for Glasgow in the morning,' said Thane, feeling his way carefully. 'Will you go with him?'

'No. I'm travelling with the bus party. We're leaving early on Sunday morning, which will get us there in plenty of time.' Dave Anderson looked at him and frowned. 'And if you're worried about what's likely to happen at the rally, don't. I told you before, nobody's going to start a riot. We know what we want, but we don't need to go rampaging through the streets to get it.'

'No blood.' Thane paused. 'No bombs, Dave?'

For a moment he thought a flickering caution had crossed the youngster's features. Then it had gone.

'No blood, Chief Inspector. No bombs,' said Dave Anderson. His mouth tightened a little. 'You've got my word on that.'

'Would Adam Jennings like to hear you taking that line?' asked Thane.

Anderson smiled, didn't comment, and nodded towards the workbench. 'I'd like to get on with this,' he said mildly.

'Then I promised Sylvia I'd look round at her place for a meal.'

Thane rubbed his chin, took the hint, and started for the door.

'Chief Inspector . . .'

'Yes?' He stopped with his hand on the handle, suddenly hopeful.

'Good night,' said Dave Anderson.

There seemed no particular reason to hurry back. A feeling inside him that he'd been talking to Dave Anderson in one language and somehow getting answers in another, Colin Thane walked wearily across the village square, reached the Clachan Arms, and glanced at his watch. In another couple of minutes the bar would be open.

The temptation was strong.

He swore, turned towards the doorway, then heard a sharp, familiar whistle. Looking round, he saw Phil Moss hurrying towards him.

'Found you . . .' Moss was slightly breathless.

'At the right moment.' Thane jerked his head towards the hotel bar. 'I'll buy.'

'Later,' said Moss firmly. 'You'll want to, I'll bet on it. But right now we'd better head back.'

'Something happened?' Thane tensed.

'Old MacMaster – or at least he's part of it,' agreed Moss happily. 'The pleasure of your company is requested. That's if you want to hear why the Marquis was shot.'

'If I . . .' Thane's mouth fell open.

Then he was on his way.

Chapter Eight

Professor Andrew MacMaster made it plain that he wasn't going to be hurried. Standing with his back to a wall-map, he had the centre of the stage, knew it, and liked it.

'Not that the – ah – idea behind what we've discovered was in any way my own,' he said deprecatingly, with a mild undertone which suggested he'd probably have come up with it anyway, given a little time. 'The credit belongs to Detective Inspector Elliot.'

'Ach, only because I was raised on a farm.' Jonas Elliot rubbed a self-conscious hand across his paunch and grinned awkwardly. 'A County man might not be of much use at some of the things you meet around a city, Chief Inspector.'

'Exactly,' murmured MacMaster. 'We all have our minor weaknesses.'

Colin Thane nodded impatiently. They were in the station main office. An oddly embarrassed Margaret Linton was in a chair nearby while Elliot leaned against a filing cabinet in one corner. As the last arrivals, he and Moss found themselves in the middle of the floor, facing Mac-Master like two overgrown schoolboys.

MacMaster considered him with an irritating amusement. 'I should also say that Miss Linton's professional ability is not put in question by the situation. In fact, the findings are as much from her veterinary knowledge as from my own confirming investigation.' He waved Margaret Linton's protest down. 'Thane, you've considered several possible motives behind the shooting of this bull. Including that it was this fellow Sam Hodge, whose gun was used. Do any of them even halfway satisfy you?'

'None,' admitted Thane. 'But . . .'

'Patience,' said MacMaster dryly. 'If Miss Linton and I can spend close to an hour working in singularly cold surroundings you can let us present the results in a proper fashion.' He glanced at the woman. 'And – ah – incidentally, it was Miss Linton, who, without knowing it, gave Elliot his idea.' Suddenly, his finger stabbed. 'Moss, tell me why those American buyers were willing to pay such a vast sum for this animal.'

Moss shrugged. 'To improve their own herds, I suppose. That's the usual reason.'

'Because they saw in the animal a magnificent piece of breeding stock,' agreed MacMaster happily. 'An animal which, as cattle experts, they'd seen and approved.' He paused and shook his head with a mock solemnity. 'However, like sensible businessmen, they'd appreciate that the animal had matured since then. They'd have a skilled professional veterinary assessment carried out when it arrived in the United States. And they would have rejected the animal out of hand.'

Thane stared at him, startled. 'Why?'

'For an excellent reason,' murmured MacMaster. 'The animal was sterile. Sadly incapable of carrying out its primary purpose.'

'Eh?' Phil Moss swallowed. 'You mean . . .'

'Exactly,' agreed MacMaster with an acid encouragement. 'It couldn't father any baby bulls, if such a child-like phrase makes the situation clearer.'

Elliot eased forward from the filing cabinet, nodding. 'Remember Miss Linton said the Marquis was a gentle beast, eh? Well, that happens and can mean nothing. But we'd a bull which was that way at home once. Ach, there

167

was damn all we could do except sell it for carcase beef.'

Thane rubbed a hand across his forehead, frowning, a whole interlocking pattern of possibilities suddenly fitting, making sense.

'But we checked through MacGhee's files,' protested Phil Moss. 'He was District Veterinary Inspector. He'd given the brute a clean bill of health!'

'Quite,' snapped MacMaster. 'But if I must put things crudely for you, the animal couldn't have fathered a pound of sausagemeat. What Miss Linton and I achieved could hardly be termed a full autopsy. But it was enough to give a positive picture.'

'He's right,' said Margaret Linton almost wearily. 'I got as big a surprise as anyone – I told you John did almost everything involving the Export Certificate tests on the Marquis. But whatever the files say, John must have known.'

'And known that the truth would come out the moment the animal was re-examined by the buyers,' said Thane with a slow nod of understanding. 'Well, there's an easy enough reason.'

'The insurance,' grated Moss suddenly. He snapped finger and thumb together. 'It was a straight death policy.'

For three-quarters of that 120,000-dollar purchase price. And for Adam Jennings three-quarters would be a considerable advance forward on nothing. Thane lit a cigarette almost without being aware of it, thinking on.

If Sam Hodge had got wind there was something wrong with the Marquis and had to be silenced, if the .38 revolver had been found among his things when they'd been collected from the cottage – then Jennings had a ready-made way out, a suspect lined up in the shape of his 'dismissed' cattleman.

With a bonus appearing when Charlie Fenn had gone blundering around the Broomvale farmyard. He wondered briefly if the killing had originally been planned for that night, or if Tommy Dougan seeing Fenn had caused it to be shaped then and there.

But that still left John MacGhee.

'MacGhee might have talked,' mused Moss, as if mind-reading. 'Sooner or later he might have talked.'

It still left gaps, areas which came down to guesswork. Yet for the first time Colin Thane felt the relief of knowing that he had a positive framework, a basic understanding. The rest could come.

He saw Elliot still grinning happily and decided he might as well get the rest of the situation out in the open.

'Nice going, Elliot,' he said mildly. 'Well, now I suppose it's my turn. We've been working on another angle.'

'Sir?' Elliot raised a puzzled eyebrow.

'The armoury raid.' Thane told it briefly, trying to ignore the County man's barely hidden indignation at having been left out. When he'd finished, it was MacMaster who broke the silence with the bright interest of a detached observer.

'So your theory is that when Adam Jennings holds his rally on Sunday his speech will either admit that the Children of the Mist claim credit for destroying some target or claim that the destruction had their support?'

'Yes.'

Detective Inspector Elliot looked at them both for a moment then sighed. 'Suddenly I've stopped feeling so clever,' he admitted sadly. 'But what do we do about it?'

'Right now, we wait.' Thane turned to Margaret Linton, a new problem on his mind. 'Any chance of Adam Jennings hearing that you've been taking a closer look at the Marquis?'

She shook her head. 'I doubt it. The butcher shop was busy – I simply told Allison the Professor wanted another look at the bullet wound.'

Thane suppressed a wry chuckle. 'Which ties in nicely.

Just about an hour ago I told Jennings he could cremate the carcase tomorrow.'

'Which must have made him happy,' said MacMaster with a frankly incredulous sniff. 'Did you mean it?'

Thane made his shrug suitably non-committal, not particularly certain himself.

'But why can't you just go and arrest him now?' demanded Margaret Linton, openly bewildered.

'Evidence,' explained Moss. He took a bismuth tablet, ignored the frown she gave him, and popped it into his mouth. 'What we know is one thing. What the courts would need is another – we can't nail him on anything yet.'

'Which is why Phil and I are planning a visit to the farm tonight,' said Thane softly. 'If we're lucky, then . . .'

Moss gave a thunderous belch.

Which was as good a comment as any.

The next few hours dragged their way round the police station clock.

They ate sandwiches brought in by Sergeant Imrie, drank coffee, talked desultorily, and kept coming back to glancing at that clock.

At 10 p.m. Detective Inspector Elliot took the late press conference. Beating off all questions with a sturdy refusal to go beyond repeating that the search was continuing for Sam Hodge, he left each and every reporter with the unqualified impression that there was a set of handcuffs ready and waiting for the vanished cattleman.

The press team left.

By midnight there had been another telephone call from Buddha Ilford. The city C.I.D. chief was in an anxious, restless mood – which was to pattern. County Headquarters had taken the same line and had had to be fought off. Ilford's contribution was small but at least reassuring. The Glasgow committee of the Children of the Mist were behaving in an apparently normal manner. And the secur-

ity searches carried out at each building on the Special
Branch list of potential targets had yielded nothing.

Colin Thane left it another half-hour, then he stubbed his
cigarette in the already overflowing ashtray, nodded at
Moss, and rose.

'I still wouldn't mind coming along,' said Detective
Inspector Elliot hopefully. He glanced at MacMaster and
Margaret Linton for support. 'I know the roads around
here.'

'We know the only one we need,' said Thane mildly.
'And someone's got to be handy here in case things go
wrong.'

'Ach, to hell with it,' declared Elliot, subsiding gloomily.
'Thane, chief inspector or no chief inspector, next time
I catch you in my parish I – I'll damn well run you in for
loitering. That's a promise.'

It was a dark night outside with plenty of cloud, a hint
of rain and minimal moonlight. They used the police Mini,
Thane driving, Moss yawning a little beside him in the
passenger seat. The village was behind them and they
were more than halfway to Broomvale Farm before Moss
spoke.

'Got a cigarette?' he asked suddenly.

Thane grinned, took a hand from the wheel, found his
pack and matches, and handed them over. 'I thought you'd
stopped.'

'That's right.' Moss stuck a cigarette in his mouth and
lit it defiantly. 'Colin, I was thinking. Suppose we grab
Jennings and make it stick – what happens to Sunday's
rally?'

'It could end up a riot.' Thane kept his eyes on the road.
'Why?'

Moss shrugged. 'Just that maybe we'll be there to find
out.'

Thane shook his head. 'Not if I can help it.' That was one
job he didn't want to know about. The Group Disorder
vehicle squads were welcome to it.

He slowed the car as they neared the Broomvale Farm turn-off, then bumped it on to the grass verge and stopped in behind a thick clump of bushes.

'We walk?' queried Moss glumly as engine and lights were switched off.

'Call it exercise,' suggested Thane.

Moss called it something else, pungently.

Five minutes on foot down the inky darkness of the tree-lined farm road brought them within sight of their object-ive. The old castle-farmhouse was a dim silhouette against the night sky, no lights at its windows, no sign of move-ment anywhere around.

They circled cautiously over the rough ground, came round below the cattle pens, and stopped for a moment. The wind brought an occasional snort as one of the Angus bulls stirred in its sleep, but the rear of the farmhouse was in the same total darkness as the front.

'All clear,' muttered Moss, shivering in the cold. 'Let's get on with it.'

Thane nodded. The conical roof of the dovehouse was just ahead. As they neared it something large and feath-ered rose suddenly from near the peak and flapped silently away.

Moss swore to himself and licked his lips.

'An owl,' said Thane dryly.

'I didn't think it was a flaming elephant,' muttered Moss. He preferred the kind of two-legged wild life that hid out in tenement alleys. With them, at least, he knew how to cope.

There was only one door to the dovecote and no win-dows. Thane used a carefully shielded flashlight for a second and gave a humourless smile as it clicked off. The dovecote door was of heavy, planked wood with a mas-sive, old-fashioned lock. But the doorpost into which the lock tongued was warped and cracked.

'The easy way?' queried Moss quietly. One hand went

into his coat pocket and brought out a tyre lever he'd borrowed from the Mini's tool kit. 'Nothing like brute strength and ignorance.'

'My idea, my door . . .' Thane took the tyre lever, slipped its thinnest end between door and post just below the lock in jemmy style, tried some pressure, and felt the old wood give a little. 'Well, let's find out.'

He levered two-handed, building up the pressure gradually, hearing the wood creak, the creak become a groan then a muted crackle. Still he kept the pressure building, avoiding the kind of sudden jerk which would have done the job quicker but with a lot more noise.

There was a final, grating protest, a sharp, momentary splintering, and the dovecote door swung open.

Behind them, a bull bellowed once then fell silent. They waited in the shadow of the tower, eyes and ears straining against the night. Nothing moved, no lights appeared at the farmhouse. After another minute, Thane gave a murmur of satisfaction and nudged Moss on.

The inside of the dovecote smelled both damp and musty. Thane closed the door behind them carefully then shone the torch around. It showed only bare stone walls and, to one side, a debris of rotted timber piled on the earth floor.

Moss crossed over to the timber, dragged some of the top pieces away, scowled down at the result, then gave a grunt of triumph. Quickly, happily now, he removed the rest of the rotted wood.

'Jackpot time,' he declared, standing back.

The piled timbers had masked a low, coffin-shaped recess in the stone wall, part of the original structure and perhaps once used to store grain. Inside it nestled a quartet of oblong metal boxes, boxes in War Department green with white stencilled lettering on their sides. Lettering which spelled out just two words.

'Dem. Charges.'

Dem. for Demolition.

Thane helped carry the boxes out into the middle of the floor. He opened the nearest, looked inside, and felt his mouth suddenly dry. Taped together in bundles of five, the stubby tubes of nitrostarch explosive lay dull and menacing in the torchlight.

The other boxes were the same. And Moss had found something else, a canvas haversack which held several more rolls of securing tape and a carefully packed bundle of acid-action pencil fuses.

'I'll need some help,' said Moss, back at the coffin niche and beckoning.

He went over and helped drag out the big, old-fashioned tin trunk which had been right at the back. On its lid were the initials 'S.H.'

'Sam Hodge,' said Thane quietly. 'Like you said, jackpot time.'

He clicked the trunk's catches, ready to swing back the lid.

And at the same moment the dovecote door slammed open.

They swung round, then froze.

'Stay very still,' warned Adam Jennings from behind the business end of a double-barrelled shotgun, his bulky figure filling the doorway. 'That's right – now up on your feet, slowly.'

As they obeyed he came in, the strong, bold-nosed face stony in the dim torchlight, the shotgun held at hip level and pointed steadily in their direction. 'Dougan . . .'

Tommy Dougan appeared behind him. The fair-haired head cattleman also had a shotgun but it was cradled under one arm and in his free hand he carried a small battery lantern. Once inside, he heeled the door shut, switched on the lantern, and laid it on the trunk.

The brilliant light filled the dovecote's gloomy interior. Adam Jennings looked first at the demolition charge boxes, then at the trunk, and turned to Thane with ice-cold eyes.

174

'You found them,' he said abruptly. 'And we found you. How does that leave things?'

'Embarrassing all round,' admitted Thane wryly. He took a vague half-step forward, saw Jennings' knuckles whiten a fraction round the shotgun, and went no further. 'I didn't see any burglar alarms.'

Dougan chuckled, a cynical, humourless sound.

'The cattle were restless,' said Jennings. 'Dougan came out to see why.' His lips twisted, a mocking note entered his voice. 'Of course you closed the door before you used that torch. But you forgot this is a dovecote, forgot the old entry-holes for the doves. From the farmhouse, this place looked like it had a party going on inside.'

Moss swore under his breath.

The shotgun's twin barrels twitched upward in command, words unnecessary. They raised their hands and Dougan came round behind them, patting their clothes in a perfunctory search. He found the tyre lever and Moss's baton, threw them aside, then moved clear.

'You can lower your hands. Then back against the wall,' ordered Jennings. He waited till they'd reached it, then frowned. 'Now the problem is exactly what to do with you.'

'And any others around,' murmured Thane.

Almost lazily, Jennings glanced at his companion. Dougan gave a fractional headshake.

'Dougan says no,' said Jennings blandly, standing with his feet apart, and an unworried confidence in his manner. 'I'll take his word for it. He's – well, more experienced in the practicalities.'

'A lot more,' agreed Moss acidly. 'That's why he's a five-time loser.'

Jennings raised an interested eyebrow. 'So you know that much. And what else brought you here?'

Thane shrugged. 'If you want a catalogue it could take some time. Suppose we start off with one sterile bull – and how you paid off MacGhee for his help.' He nodded

175

towards the tin trunk. 'One thing we don't know is what you did with Sam Hodge.'

Not a muscle moved on Jennings' face and he didn't answer. The grey eyes stared at Thane, without anger but with something more deadly – a completely detached thoughtfulness.

'The longer we hang around like this . . .' began Dougan, openly on edge. He didn't finish, but swallowed hard. A small, moth-like insect buzzed into the lantern's glare and stayed there circling madly around the glass.

'We'll pull out,' said Jennings suddenly. 'I'll bring the car down, we'll load the charges aboard, and get clear before anyone wonders about these two.'

Relieved, Dougan grunted agreement. 'And them?'

'We'll have to be practical. Take over.' Jennings waited till Dougan's shotgun had lined up then stooped over the nearest box and carefully lifted one of the taped bundles of charges. 'Now, if we used a delayed action fuse . . .'

Dougan's shotgun quivered a little, but he nodded. 'I could rig one. It would go off in about an hour.'

'And the bang would bring half the countryside running – not to mention your housekeeper,' reminded Thane. He felt fear crawling inside him, knew Adam Jennings wasn't bluffing. But there was nothing he could do but stand and cling to hope. Too often he'd seen the size of hole a close-range shotgun could blow in a man's middle.

'I gave my housekeeper the weekend off,' said Jennings calmly. 'That was chance – a lucky one. And noise – well, that's what I want. Noise and a diversion. If your friends arrive and have to dig through a heap of stones to find out what's happened they won't have time for anything else.' He smiled, no viciousness attached to the words, his manner casually matter of fact. 'Of course, it means nobody will hear that speech I had ready. A pity – but the rest can stay unchanged.'

'Bombs for Freedom week?' asked Thane, his voice hoarse.

'Something like that,' murmured Jennings. 'Interested in what the rest of these charges will accomplish?'

Thane managed to nod.

'We're going to destroy the main generator station at the Tummel-Garry hydro dam.' Jennings paused, waiting his reaction.

Thane said nothing. He'd have won that bet Ilford offered. But not with much chance of collecting. Well, at least Special Branch would be waiting there. Which was better than nothing.

Dougan snickered nervously and glanced at Jennings.

It was Phil Moss's chance and he took it. He plunged forward, grabbing for the shotgun – but a fraction of a second too late. Dougan moved faster, side-stepped, stuck out a foot which sent Moss lurching off balance, then swung the weapon in an upward butt-stroke. It took Moss hard on the side of the head. He seemed to crumple rather than fall then hit the cold earth floor and lay motionless.

It had happened and was over before Thane could move. And Adam Jennings already had the other shotgun lined up on his chest.

'I should have thumped him harder,' grated Dougan bitterly.

Tight-lipped, ignoring them, Thane crossed over and stooped down. Blood trickled from a gash high on Moss's temple. But he was still breathing.

'On your feet,' said Jennings impatiently.

Reluctantly, Thane obeyed and was prodded back against the wall. Jennings sighed and considered him with something close to a scowl.

'Keep him there,' he ordered Dougan. 'And don't take your eyes off him.'

He turned and stalked out into the night, dragging the door shut behind him. Dougan grunted to himself then sat on the tin trunk beside the lantern, casting a black shadow on the opposite wall.

'I'd say he's three-parts crazy,' said Thane flatly. He

waited, got no answer, and studied the man. Dougan was nervous all right – nervous and worried. You could often push a nervous man. But the trouble was you never knew which way. 'Ever killed anyone before, Dougan?'

'No,' snapped Dougan. He managed a broken-toothed leer. 'But a couple o' cops would be a good way to start.'

'Which means you were only the back-up boy when Hodge and MacGhee were killed,' murmured Thane. He scratched his head and smiled fleetingly at the way the shotgun quivered. 'You've strayed out of your league, Dougan. Thief, yes – and a few other things. But you're no fanatic. One of those bulls outside probably knows as much about politics as you do – and cares as little. So why tie in with Adam Jennings? How did he find you, anyway?'

'He knows some people. They know me.'

Dougan shrugged uneasily 'Go ahead, talk your head off if you want. Makes no odds to me – or you, now.'

Colin Thane glanced over at Moss, still lying motionless then back to Dougan. For the next two or three minutes this solitary thug held both their lives in his grimy hands. Held their lives – and all he had to work with was words.

'Let's talk then,' he said calmly. 'Does Jennings pay well?' It drew no answer and he tried again. 'He won't any more. The cupboard's gone bare – you know that. Getting the insurance from the Marquis claim was his last hope. And when you're with him on the run – well, watch your back. You could be top of the list if he decides to economize.'

It got home. Dougan licked his lips and snarled, 'He'll pay. He needs me.'

For a moment Thane didn't answer, almost forgot he was there. Behind Dougan the door of the dovecote had just eased open a couple of exploratory inches, eased, stopped, then gently closed again. Somebody had to be out there, somebody who might help. If he could give them the chance. His brain unfroze again and he grinned pityingly.

'The tame explosives expert,' he mocked. 'Hasn't he always been around when you've been assembling those charges – been around, asking questions, learning?'

'Shut up,' hissed Dougan. 'I know this kind o' game, and I'm not playing.'

'You'd rather string along with a fanatic who's a killer?' Thane shook his head. 'He'll keep you for this job, maybe even the next. If there is a next. Then . . .'

He stopped short as a sudden scraping, rustling sound came from the wall to Dougan's right. A cloud of dust and debris shot from one of the old bird-entries – then a close-packed wad of blazing straw. The straw hit the floor and scattered, flaming and smoking, spraying towards the demolition charge boxes.

Dougan sprang to his feet at the same instant as the dovecote door burst open. Mouth framing a curse, he swung round wildly and triggered the shotgun. The booming blast of shot scoured an empty doorway and, wide-eyed, he tried to slew round again.

At which exact instant Thane catapulted across the gap between them, one hand grabbing the gun and levering its menace towards the roof, the other seizing in a throat-hold. They crashed down on the earth floor, rolling on the burning straw, Thane transformed into an ice-cold, merciless fighting machine – a machine which knew this had to be finished quickly.

His right knee came up hard and low in the man's stomach, bringing a half-choked gobble of pain. The shotgun fell loose, Dougan's arms clawed wildly. And Thane transferred both hands to the man's shoulders, jerking him round, the smell of unwashed clothing strong in his nostrils.

It was the prelude to the most effective of the Glasgow

179

ned's back-street tricks – a slamming head-butt against Dougan's face.

Dougan screamed. Thane hit him once more, a double-fisted chop behind the left ear. And the man went limp.

Panting, Thane sank back on his heels and realized for the first time there were other people now beside him – three figures busily stamping out the last traces of the smouldering straw. One of them stopped, turned and winked at him.

'Sorry we kept you waiting,' said Dave Anderson. 'We'd the devil of a job finding a pole to push that straw through.'

Thane sucked a deep breath, swallowed hard, then remembered. 'Jennings – he'd hear the shot.'

'Hold on.' Anderson whistled shrilly and a head looked briefly round the doorway from outside. 'Any sign, Tubby?'

The fat-faced youngster concerned shook his head and vanished again. Rising to his feet, Thane remembered where he'd seen him before – and the others. They were the trio who'd been at the workshop hut.

'You followed us?'

'No.' One of his companions was already bending over Moss. Another had the shotgun. Anderson gestured towards the demolition charges. 'We came to try and find these – to get rid of them.'

Later it might make sense. But for the moment he had to trust them. Trust them and stop Adam Jennings. Thane saw the tyre lever lying on the floor, picked it up, and turned for the door.

'I'm coming,' volunteered Anderson.

'If it isn't too late,' said Thane grimly.

'His car won't start,' Anderson told him calmly. 'We cut the spark-plug leads, just in case things went wrong.'

They headed out and hurried towards the farmhouse. The cattle enclosures were noisy with snorting, frightened beasts, dark shapes which fled to the far side of their pens as Thane and Anderson passed. Then, as they neared the farmhouse, Thane heard a new sound – the rapid, desperate turning of a starter motor. A moment later he saw the car ahead, the driver's door half-opened.

He began to run, conscious of Anderson close by his side. When the starter motor died, the headlamps suddenly flared to life, pinning them in their beams. Behind those lights – Thane swung desperately, shoved Dave Anderson sprawling, then dived for the dirt himself.

The twin blasts of the shotgun almost merged. A hail of pellets scythed the night and in an instant the cattle around had erupted into bellowing, madly rushing panic. Already up again, Thane sprinted for the car.

A second for Jennings to break open that gun. Say two more to extract the used shells, two, maybe three more to reload . . .

He reached the car as the first fresh shell was being punched in. Jennings saw him coming, tried feverishly to close the breech, failed, switched his grip, and swung the shotgun back like a club.

For Colin Thane it had all happened a hundred times before, ever since he'd been a beat cop with a baton still learning that there were pages in the rulebook you had to leave behind at police college.

Timed to perfection, the tyre lever chopped down as Jennings' muscular arms reached the full extent of their backswing. The cold metal jarred in Thane's hand as it smashed the bone of that exposed left elbow.

Jennings gave a high, almost womanish scream of pain. Somehow he managed to throw the gun at Thane, then he was running with that left arm hanging limp and useless. Stumbling over the gun, Thane lost a few yards as he followed down a narrow lane leading through the noisy confusion of cattle pens.

The gap began to close. Jennings looked back once, forced an even faster pace, and suddenly the cloud-filtered moonlight showed a dead end ahead where the lane ended in still another pen. Reaching it, the man clambered through and ran again. Thane made to follow – but came to a horrified halt with one leg through.

Only a few yards ahead Adam Jennings had come to a halt. A great black shape, mouth foam-flecked, was moving towards him from the far side of the pen.

For a second Jennings hesitated then swung to come back. It was too late. Charging like some panic-maddened mountain, the massive Angus bull smashed him down and went over him in a flurry of trampling fury.

Still smarting from the last encounter it had had with humans, the Earl of Broomvale travelled a few more snorting, head-tossing yards then spun, bellowed once, and thundered back as Adam Jennings tried to crawl for the fence. It reached him, slammed once, twice, with its great, blunt head, then began a systematic pounding with its forelegs.

A final snort of triumph and it trotted away, leaving a broken, moaning shape bleeding in the mud.

Powerless till then, his throat hoarse from useless shouting, Colin Thane dived through, grabbed Jennings by the shoulders, and dragged him clear. At the fence, a white-faced Dave Anderson helped him lift Jennings through. As they did, the bull came trotting back, bellowed again, then turned away.

Stripping off his coat, Thane used it as a pillow for Adam Jennings' blood-streaked, muddied head. Beside him, Dave Anderson looked closer at the dark-haired giant's broken body then turned away, gagging.

'Thane –' the name came as a whisper from Jennings' pain-racked lips – 'you wanted to know about Hodge. You might – might as well, now.'

Colin Thane bent over the man, knew there was no sense in denying it, and nodded.

Jennings smiled fleetingly, almost wearily. 'He found out about – about the Marquis. He'd have talked. I –' he

182

coughed, and blood appeared on his lips – 'I couldn't afford that. So I killed him.'

'Where is he?' asked Thane softly.

'Buried in – in one of the fields. Dougan knows.' The man took a shallow, whistling breath. 'Get the rest straight too, eh? MacGhee . . .'

'It can wait,' said Thane almost gruffly.

The dark head shook a little. 'MacGhee phoned. Said – said he'd clubbed Inspector Fenn – was in a panic. So I – I went over. Fenn was still unconscious. John was weak – too weak. Everything seemed made to – to measure. Even the knife.' His voice faded away, then he peered past Thane. 'Dave – is that . . .'

'I'm here,' said Dave Anderson quietly. The redhead came closer, stooping over him. 'I'm sorry, Adam.'

'We – never did agree much,' murmured Jennings, forcing that same smile again. 'My way went wrong. Your way . . .'

'I'll still try,' said Anderson gravely. 'But my way, Adam. Only my way. Not yours.'

'Better than –' Jennings grimaced hard – 'better than none. But . . .' He didn't finish. His body gave one spasmodic quiver then was still.

'That's it, Dave,' said Thane quietly. He laid his hand on the young redhead's shoulder and nodded.

Anderson rose slowly to his feet and drew a deep breath. 'That's it,' he echoed, then shrugged and turned away.

The cattle pens were gradually quietening as they walked back. In the background the old tall walls of the castle-farmhouse seemed to brood in silhouette against the night sky. Thane ignored it all, quickening his step as they neared the dovecote.

Then he slowed and gave a crinkling grin of relief. Bright light streamed from the dovecote doorway. Phil Moss was waiting there, pale and wan but on his feet.

They'd been lucky, luckier than any two cops had the right to expect.

Twenty minutes later D.I. Elliot and Sergeant Imrie arrived with a squad of uniformed men. So did MacMaster and Margaret Linton. Leaning against a fence post, Thane smoked a cigarette and watched as a dazed, handcuffed Tommy Dougan was loaded aboard a patrol van and driven off. It would come back. There was another cargo waiting – a stretcher with the mangled, bloodied body of Adam Jennings mercifully covered by a blanket.

He felt a nudge at his side, turned, and met a weak grin from Moss.

'How about getting out of here?' suggested Moss. He nodded across to where Margaret Linton was standing at the Earl of Broomvale's pen. Elliot was there too, a frown on his face as he watched the bull quietly munching from its feed trough. 'I've got – well, reasons.'

'Like what?' queried Thane innocently.

'That woman,' said Moss uneasily. He stroked the patch of adhesive dressing on his temple. 'Look, when she put this on – ach, well there's just a chance she has the wrong idea about things.'

Thane looked at him long and consideringly then invited, 'Go on.'

Moss belched unhappily. 'Colin, I'm not interested. When she gets a man she'll run him like a railway time-table – or a ruddy zoo.'

'Give me a minute,' Thane told him. Then crinkled a grin. 'You can hide in one of the cars.'

He left Moss spluttering wrathfully and walked across to Dave Anderson and his friends. They were standing a little way apart from the general activity and he signalled Anderson over.

'I wanted to say thanks, Dave.'

'No need,' said Anderson briefly. He thrust his hands into his pockets. 'You still haven't asked . . .'

184

'I will now,' interrupted Thane flatly. 'How much did you know?'

Anderson shrugged, his lean young face serious. 'Until this afternoon, nothing – except about the armoury raid. Adam told a few of us about that soon after it happened.'

'Who was in on it?'

'Adam and a couple of his Glasgow committee pals – plus Dougan, of course,' replied Anderson. He grimaced. 'He wouldn't tell us where the stuff was hidden. That meant the only way to stop him was to be here when he brought it out in the open.'

'Lucky for us,' murmured Thane. He flicked his cigarette away. 'And the rest?'

'Next to nothing – except for some pretty late guess-work.' Anderson sounded almost apologetic. 'I've a friend on the Glasgow committee – Eric Francis – we went through University together, he thinks the way I do. Eric was up with Peter Cass and Campbell yesterday.'

Thane nodded. 'I remember him.'

'Well, I phoned Eric from Pitlochry this afternoon. He told me Jennings left them for about an hour that evening, just after he'd had a telephone call. When he came back, he said he'd had to move the demolition charges in a hurry, that your people were likely to find them by acci-dent. Afterwards – well, they had to back him up and say he'd never left them. They didn't guess what had really happened.'

Thane didn't speak at once. There was still Sam Hodge. But they had Dougan and Dougan would talk now – talk as loud and as long as necessary to get himself off the hook.

That left only two questions he wanted to ask.

'Dave, did you know what he'd planned to blow up?'

'No,' answered Anderson bleakly. 'He wouldn't tell us, which made things even worse. Only that it would be something big.'

185

'It would have been.' Thane didn't go on, but switched to the other question on his mind, one not for the official report.

'What will you do now?'

'Cancel Sunday's rally, for a start,' declared Anderson, looking past him across the cattle pens into the night. 'Then . . . well, a few of us had plans made anyway. We'll clean out Jennings' pals then shape a new Children of the Mist image. That's going to be quite a public relations job after this lot. But we know what we want.'

Something in his voice made Thane raise an eyebrow. 'Meaning?'

'Hell, we don't want complete Home Rule – that's strictly for the birds,' said Anderson with a dry amusement. 'We'll shout for it, and shout loud. To get people out of their ruts, to make the politicians feel worried. But we'll work differently from the usual. None of the protest march stuff, for instance. We plan a few things. Things that will – well, surprise people yet keep them on our side. We'll stir things up until every politician who wants votes will make sure Scotland gets a real share of prosperity. They'll do it to try to shut us up – not knowing that's exactly what they're meant to do.' The grin grew wider. 'If you want the moon, ask for the stars. But repeat that anywhere and I'll call you a liar.'

Thane swallowed and wondered exactly what breed of youngster the world had coming up. Wondered – and partly envied them their prospect.

'No bombs, no riots?'

'My word on it,' said Dave Anderson gravely.

The Monday night school concert was packed with dutiful parents plus a full turn-out of teachers who smiled hard and made appropriate noises.

Colin Thane sat in the back row of the hall and relaxed. Beside him, Mary rustled her programme. On stage, a child with freckles and a violin came out and began to play.

The tune was hard to place. Maybe because his mind was wandering.

They'd spent all Saturday and Sunday mopping up. Under escort, Tommy Dougan had led a squad to where Sam Hodge was buried. The old cattleman's head had been smashed in. Peter Cass and half-a-dozen other old-guard Jennings men from around Glasgow were being held for questioning.

And the Children of the Mist had announced Dave Anderson was their new president.

Half-listening, still trying to place the tune, Thane felt a hand touch his shoulder. He looked round and saw Buddha Ilford standing behind him, beckoning. Nudging Mary, he shrugged at her frown, squeezed along the row of seats, and followed the city C.I.D. chief out into the corridor.

'Enjoying it?' asked Ilford bleakly.

'I've seen worse, sir.' Another fifteen minutes and it would be over for another year.

'No doubt.' Ilford's voice was gravel-rough but controlled. 'I took your report home this evening, read it through. Everything there . . . nearly everything.'

'Sir?'

'Everything except this.' Ilford took a folded sheet of paper from his pocket and handed it over. 'I got it twenty minutes back, an advance copy. It'll be issued to the news agencies within the hour.'

The press release was short and apologetic.

'Inland Revenue announce that owing to a technical fault of a temporary nature at Centre One, East Kilbride, all taxation business normally dealt with by Centre One will be subject to considerable delay.

'Inland Revenue regrets . . .'

Thane didn't bother with the rest.

He knew Centre One – a vast, sprawling nineteen-storey

187

complex just outside Glasgow, an electronic giant rapidly spinning a new computer tape and punched card income tax web as it swallowed up the previous work of scores of local Inland Revenue offices. If something had really gone wrong there the result would be chaos.

'It says a temporary fault.'

'I can read,' said Ilford with some exasperation. 'What it means is that since this morning their damned computers have been practically useless. Almost every programme library file tape and main master storage tape in the place has gone sour. The best explanation their boffins can offer is that someone got in last night and used some kind of electro-magnet gadget – used it to generate a magnetic field which wiped their tapes clean.

'Any ideas?'

'Not straight off,' answered Thane warily. But he groaned inwardly, remembering a workshop hut and its cluster of bits and pieces of electrical hardware.

'No?' Ilford snorted. 'Centre One had a damned great *skean dhu* knife painted six feet high on the front door when the staff arrived this morning.' He stopped and his face dissolved in an ear-to-ear grin. 'You know what this means? Inland Revenue have lost track of close on half a million tax payers. They can't send out tax codings, demand notes, anything.' He tapped his bulky chest in near delight. 'They've lost track of people like me – and every other cop in the city. It could be months before they're organized again.'

Thane swallowed hard, sensing what was coming.

'Who's handling it?'

'Odd you should ask,' mused Ilford. 'I've been ordered to give all possible assistance, which is somebody's bad luck. There's no sign of forced entry, no visible damage – just that those tapes have been wiped without being touched. Even if we prove anything, I'm damned if I know what kind of charge it will be.' He stopped and eyed

188

Thane blandly. 'You still want Detective Constable Beech off the hook for that insubordination affair?'

Thane sighed and nodded.

'It can wait till morning,' said Ilford airily.

He went away. Thane stood for a moment, eyes half-closed.

No, the new-look Children of the Mist wouldn't fight any battles in the street. They wouldn't need to, this way.

A blast of music from the hall signalled the start of the concert's grand finale. He hurried back in, reached his seat, and flopped down.

Young Tommy missed his cue and came on late. Kate dropped her wand halfway through her 'second assistant fairy' routine.

But they were up there grinning fit to burst. Suddenly he felt that way too.

Colin Thane got up on his feet at the finish and applauded like everyone else.